Cities Burn and People Die

INDEEGO

Ukiyoto Publishing

All global publishing rights are held by

Ukiyoto Publishing

Published in 2025

Content Copyright © INDEEGO

ISBN 9789370090279

All rights reserved.

No part of this publication may be reproduced, transmitted, or stored in a retrieval system, in any form by any means, electronic, mechanical, photocopying, recording or otherwise, without the prior permission of the publisher.

The moral rights of the author have been asserted.

This is a work of fiction. Names, characters, businesses, places, events, locales, and incidents are either the products of the author's imagination or used in a fictitious manner. Any resemblance to actual persons, living or dead, or actual events is purely coincidental.

This book is sold subject to the condition that it shall not by way of trade or otherwise, be lent, resold, hired out or otherwise circulated, without the publisher's prior consent, in any form of binding or cover other than that in which it is published.

www.ukiyoto.com

Dedication

A very special friend of mine, I call her 'Munchkin' because she's cute and small, she has played a pivotal role in the brightest and grimmest parts of this book, though she may not be aware of it. My sister, too, she passed away in 2007. She inspired the creation and character of Shirley.

And also to the two "dud" books I wrote that haunted me ceaselessly for months. Odyssey of the Ascension Souls and Nomfazwe & Nkosana: Element Sources and a Witch's Wrath. These two books were so embarrassingly laden with typos that I wished to erase them from existence.

I even contemplated abandoning my aspirations to become a renowned author as I had messed up not one, but TWO books. But I eventually accepted that they were out there and that there was nothing I can do about it, despite the birth of my pseudonym 'Indeego' to run away from them. The benefits of your books not being famous, I guess, dilute the embarrassment.

Now, I failed to get those two books republished, so I wrote LOVE. MAGICK. BEACONS to replace the latter, and this one, Cities Burn and People Die, to replace the former. Odd, but I sleep better now.

Contents

CHAPTER 1
A HOLOCAUST　　　　　　　　　　1
CHAPTER 2
THE SENTINELS OF ANATHEMA　　12
CHAPTER 3
ANTEBELLUM　　　　　　　　　　22
CHAPTER 4
PEPA　　　　　　　　　　　　　　31
CHAPTER 5
THE SKY CAN BLEED LEECHES　　41
CHAPTER 6
THE SKEWED BUILDING　　　　　52
CHAPTER 7
IN THE CITY　　　　　　　　　　62
CHAPTER 8
BELLUM　　　　　　　　　　　　73
CHAPTER 9
THREATS　　　　　　　　　　　　84
CHAPTER 10
HYPOCRISY　　　　　　　　　　　95
CHAPTER 11
MURDER! MURDER!　　　　　　106
CHAPTER 12

AZRAEL'S VISIT	116
CHAPTER 13	
HIS DEPRAVED DESIRES	127
CHAPTER 14	
THE FACES THEY MAKE	139
CHAPTER 15	
WEAPONS OF A BLADE CLASH TOGETHER	148
CHAPTER 16	
THE TRUTH OF IT ALL	161
CHAPTER 17	
SHIVERS	175
CHAPTER 18	
THREE IS A CROWD	185
CHAPTER 19	
EYES TO SEE, LIPS TO SMILE	197
CHAPTER 20	
HE'S DEAD, HE'S ALIVE, HE'S HOLLOW	207
CHAPTER 21	
EPITHET OF FIRE	217
CHAPTER 22	
POSTBELLUM	227
CHAPTER 23	
IT'S A SUICIDE	243
CHAPTER 24	
ODD CITY	254
About the Author	*269*

CHAPTER 1
A HOLOCAUST

"He uses us, like limbs, like teeth to chew his prey, tongues to lick his prey, mouths to manipulate them, noses to stalk them by their scent, eyes to see them suffer. He lives because there is life, for his very essence vows that as long as there are still those who breathe, he will never stop. Your death is his death. Your very lives are a declaration of war to him — and in wars, people die and cities burn."

8 YEARS EARLIER.

In the darkest of nights, the moon is absent and the clouds gather, and the only sound one can hear is their own breath and their last scream whilst a sudden sharp unbearable pain tears their soul from this world, should they not be wary and tread carefully. On this night, the silence is accompanied by screams of terror, gunshots, weeping, and the overruling sound of a raging fire crackling and charring homes.

Within the tall curtain walls, death claimed many lives in the third city as burning buildings toppled over other buildings and civilians. In the biggest and tallest building of all, in the luxurious suite at the top floor, that was where the perpetrator lurked. There was a wounded man hiding behind his bed, he had a drawer propped tightly against the doorknob. The man was bleeding profusely on his expensive purple suit, he appeared to be stabbed on his left shoulder socket, rendering his left arm useless. On his right hand he clutched an H&K MP5K. His heart was pulsating, he was panting, his face doused in sweat and expressed fear — fear of death — of his demise.

He stared in horror through his window wall at the burning city. It was impossible to fathom that this was really happening. He used to love the view of the city lights at night, his building was nearly as tall as the curtain wall around the city. He heard his remaining men shoot and swear, then the sound of sharp blades cutting through the air, then squelching and screaming. Then, it was dead silent in the suite.

He heard light, patient footsteps outside his room, not the footsteps of someone who had to kill him urgently and flee the scene before the cops arrive. This person was a psycho. When this mysterious mass murderer stabbed the man before, the man had only seen a fleeting shadow faster than the blink of an eye, but then again, he had been drinking a lot a few hours before the city turned to hell.

The footsteps stopped behind his door. He had found him. He swallowed hard, and garnered the courage to stand up and shoot hysterically at everything in that direction. He opened fire and emptied the clip, hoping to have gotten the psycho. He kept his finger pressed against the trigger even after he ran out of bullets. He was flustered. Frozen in fear, he could hear his heartbeat as clear as one would with a stethoscope.

To his surprise, the door was wide open. The drawer was smashed against the wall. He could not tell if it was opened during his fire or before that. He could not believe what was happening. Only a few people were capable of such feats, and he was in cahoots with all of them. He could not wrap his head around what had befallen him, why this person or thing was attacking them. His fear finally got the best of his knees, they weakened and he fell.

He crawled to the window wall and leaned against it, he dropped the gun and hastily reached out for the extra magazine from his waist but then stopped when he saw his trail of blood, his shins and knees had cuts, that was what had caused him to fall. He started feeling lightheaded and weak. He began sobbing and shouted, "You're going to go to hell for what you've done! You have killed many innocent people! What do you want from us?" His voice was tremulous.

The murderer showed himself, he made an abrupt appearance before the man and startled him. He was sitting on the man's bloody trail with his legs crossed.

Both his hands were on his knees — as either to prop himself or to mock the man's inert knees.

He had an abnormally wide maniacal grin with snag teeth, his circle graphite eyes were bigger than they should be. He was truly insane. He had a darkness cast over his face like a shadow which did nothing but highlight his light skin even further from his neck down. He was heavily shredded, but not bulky. He was a result of heavy lifting and CrossFit. His muscles looked as though they were metallic. He had a Zulu axe on the right side of his waist, an iklwa on the left side, a dagger on each vambrace clasped by sharp barbed wire. He was holding two gory short swords, with their sheaths crossed on his back.

He wore a breastplate with a short sleeve shirt underneath. He donned nearly slouchy pants with shin guards. His tactical boots were shiny like metal, so were his vambraces. He was 5'2, which was a detail that bothered the injured, very tall man. He wore stark black.

His midnight dreads reached down his upper back. They were spikey and seemingly solid (except when they waver as he moved quick enough), in the middle across his head down to the last tip on his upper back the dreads looked like a fish's skeletal fin. From the sides to conjoining with the middle they were protruding outward, and on the farther sides hung down like centipede legs all the way to his upper back — with two locks hanging down the left side of his forehead as a result of a habit he had before a shadow was cast over his face. Some dreads also loomed and sparsely covered his shoulders.

He laughed hysterically and replied, "Hell? You see, there are different types of people in this world. Among those types are people like me, and people like you. People like you who are scared of hell, and people like me who relish the thought of going to hell." The man was aghast.

The killer smirked and continued, "None of you are innocent. You all deserve to go to hell, I gave you all a scene of what to expect once your bodies are burned to a crisp. I know what you and your friends did." The man was confounded, the killer's strange eyes widened as he laughed aloud. "Wow, you even forgot," His entire expression shunted in a second, he narrowed his eyes at the man and angrily said, "I was there, 16 years ago."

The man caught up, he begged him, "Please, it wasn't my idea. They forced me to take over this city. I didn't have a choice."

The killer watched indifferently as the man desperately tried explaining and beg for mercy, he even offered to help the killer if he spared him. The man blinked and the killer was standing beside him, facing the window, pensively watching the city in flames continue to collapse. He quietly said, "No one forced you to do anything, you're not yourself. The screams have died down, seems most of you are dead. I'll have to go around. Make sure your friends find nothing but death. I made sure they know I did this."

The man reached for the magazine while the killer was distracted, he kept him talking. "You killed families, little kids, old people who could not defend themselves. You're no different from us. Someone will escape and-"

"I did, I will make sure every single one of you is dead. I don't discriminate, you all had it coming. I know those little demons and old demons of yours are also part of it. You declared war, and you should know in wars people die and cities burn. Another difference between people like you and people like me is, people like you start wars to murder whoever to win and come out on top, people like me, well, we keep the war going for as long as possible without a care of who wins or loses, if there are still people breathing, we won't stop — and that's why people like me don't like to start fights, but people like you like to start fights. I burned the code to the gate wall, so no one will escape. You see, I'm not like you, I'm worse than you."

The man quickly inserted the magazine and aimed at the killer and fired. He died instantaneously before he could see what happened. He believed his bleeding caught up to him and he used his last strength to kill the mass murderer. But what happened was before he could shoot, his hand was sliced off and was used to shoot him in the head, emptied the clip, too, even though he died on the first bullet.

The city the mysterious being had burned to the ground was one of the 35 cities under the Sentinels of Anathema. The Sentinels of Anathema were humans who had supernatural abilities bestowed upon them by an obscure deity called Anathema. The Sentinels of Anathema had obtained their powers nearly two decades ago when the sky bled on this small world. Millions died that day. The Sentinels bound together and summoned Anathema to spare the world in return they would appease his anger by protecting humans and ensuring they stay on a path that does not suppress Mother Nature, thus humans now lived in their cities surrounded by curtain walls to avoid sullying the earth, but they were not restricted within their cities.

The Sentinels of Anathema was made up of six members: Amanirenas, Yoddha, Bullpit, Athanasy, The Jackal, and Stomper, who were supposed to be the only ones to have attained such power over their fellow humans. But with the precipitous emergence of a new, mysterious being, a villainous being without a conscience, it would seem there was an error in Anathema's blessings, or perhaps the being was tied to the Sentinels of Anathema in a thread that could be traced to the past.

The following the day, in one of the neighboring cities.

Athanasy was visiting one of their cities to conduct some official business, she had a penthouse of her own, as did all the other five members of the group in every city. They were revered as deities. Feared as deities. Worshipped in shrines and had statues of them built in every single city. She had been preoccupied writing her cursed book when she was called for an urgent matter to the tower that required her immediate attention. This had angered her, but her anger was redirected when they played a footage for her of a city being burned down and each civilian being brutally murdered.

"How did it get here? Who filmed it?" She asked the twelve leaders of the city dressed in suits, one of them answered, "One of the guards at the tall gate said it was dropped from the sky," they seemed terrified. She was quiet. She watched intently, it was hard to keep up with the events of the film, the person who recorded it was moving exceedingly fast, indubitably not an ordinary human. The leaders of the city were terrified seeing another being with supernatural abilities, especially one that was evil. The boardroom was quiet, except for the chaos in the film. The screams and cries of the people getting slaughtered in the film were traumatic.

It hit Athanasy, she had an idea of what could be happening, but she was reserved. Towards the end of the film, before running toward this city, the mass murderer recording the film gave them a broader view of the burning city, he even laughed joyfully, he was taunting them. The leaders were appalled. No human could climb the walls, they were hundreds of feet high and they were smooth and straight.

Then, as he continued recording this horror, he ran to this city and climbed the curtain wall using his weapons. At the top of the wall, he put the camera down and walked into the shot, he waved at the camera with a maniacal smile. As if there were any doubts, he had the same power as the Sentinels, he gave them the finger before kicking the camera down the wall for the guards at the tall gate to find.

The film ended, the tension from Athanasy affected those in the room, she was fuming with indignation. One of them asked her if there were more like her and the others out there, Athanasy did not answer her, she remained quiet, who knew what was going on inside her head.

"Those powers... they are like The Jackal's..."

"Is Anathema creating an evil version of the Sentinels?"

"Is he related to The Jackal?"

Another one, her voice trembling, "Athanasy, you will protect us from this monster, right? He has nothing on the Sentinels of Anathema, right?" Everyone waited for a reassuring response from her.

She swiveled from the blank screen and faced them with a neutral expression on her face, she could see in their eyes they were one sentence away from breaking into a frenzy. She calmly told them, "I cannot deal with this, I will relay this to the other members, then we will get to the bottom of this together. Don't let anyone else hear of what happened, we cannot have the city panicking. Tell the guards at the gates to keep their mouths shut. The Sentinels will go out and hunt this sadistic fake and bring him to justice." There, their faces, they were reassured. The Sentinels of Anathema would never fail them.

Athanasy was spellbinding, she was a true paradigm of a salacious goddess. She was very stimulating, her body jiggled to the slightest of movements. She donned a very sheer red dress without sleeves, it was easy to get views from the front and both sides. The front view and the side views were not the only things to feast one's eyes upon, her dress had a crisscross slit which exposed her curves and thick thighs.

Besides her body, her face was another mesmerizing thing about her, she had the prettiest face imaginable with seductive, listless eyes. She wore pearls with glowing purple cursed symbols in each pearl, no one understood the symbols except her, she wore red high heels with the ankle strap. She made men fall in love with her without even using her mind powers. Between her black-suffused eyes were black vertical runic symbols spelling Athanasy using the runic alphabets, even under her eyes were runic short words. Her skin was literally gold. She was the only Sentinel of Anathema with gold skin. She was 5'9. She had long charcoal hair that covered most of her exposed back. She was a "problem".

She was rumored to be the most dangerous of the Sentinels of Anathema, beside her was the most powerful — Stomper. She had unfathomable etheric power that knew no bounds, she was infamous for her mind abilities, she could plant false life-long memories in one's head, cause hallucinations, get inside someone's head, induce a drunk or high state, but those were just the ones the public knew of – there were so many horrific things she could do.

There was a rumor that circulated that she once had an affair with one of the big shots in an undisclosed city, after she found out he was being unfaithful she used her magic to make him disembowel himself and watched him gulp his organs. The former lover could not die as it was one of Athanasy's tricks to move the soul from one's body, she had trapped his soul in his body when he was supposed to die, after the harrowing events, she eventually let him go, but he was by that time a demented spirit.

People dismissed that story as nothing but a story made up by the immense fear she had built inside people due to her unbridled powers, and also because they could not wrap their heads around a sane man cheating on such a goddess. I shall not dwell on their supposed relationship any longer as this is not a love story.

CHAPTER 2
THE SENTINELS OF ANATHEMA

After the attack on one of the Sentinels of Anathema's cities, Athanasy granted the police department a permit to go investigate at the scene for anything that could lead to them tracing the mass murderer and sent out troops to find and recover anything useful that may be salvaged. There was no need to search for survivors, there weren't any, the mysterious being had slaughtered every single person in that city, the film had also shown him sneaking into the bunkers, there was a glitchy moment before he blew all the bunkers up. Tours outside the curtain walls from the 31 cities were suspended indefinitely.

Hours later, Athanasy heard loud cheers throughout the city, the other members were arriving. It sounded like a parade outside. She had called them and filled them in on everything that had taken place, but she had not relayed to them the entire film's contents. She had sat alone in the Sentinels' own private boardroom at the top of the tower watching the film over and over for hours, contemplating, analyzing the mass murderer's moves. He intentionally did not film the part where he murdered those in the suite, and the part where he reveals why he was doing all of this, solely to confuse the Sentinels of Anathema.

The first one to arrive was Amanirenas, she flew above the city and knocked on the window, everyone on the ground was screaming her name, she waved down with a genuine smile but could not wait to get into the boardroom and get to the bottom of this mess. Then one by one the members arrived until everyone was present. The noise outside did not stop, the people of the city were having a sudden parade to celebrate all Sentinels being in one place at the same time – this had not happened in a while.

Stomper could not wait any longer or waste time on greetings, he demanded the video be played at once. Stomper was no doubt the most frightening to look at, and implicitly crowned the leader of the Sentinels of Anathema, by himself. But his frightening demonic appearance was used in an apotropaic manner. Though, the kids, they had to be taught not to fear his stuff of nightmares appearance. Too many reported nightmares of him feasting on their parents, it nearly led the cities down a dark path, but ignorance could always be battled with knowledge.

Stomper was large. He was an amalgam of obesity and muscularity. He had a potbelly. His skin was charred, his veins were vessels of lava, his eyes were seas of blood, his teeth were as black as coal, and were, typically, snaggy. His canines were curled outward, like tusks, which hindered him from ever really closing his mouth. He was bald, with two protruding bull horns on the sides of his cranium. His face was so creased. The size of his fists and bare feet were frightening. He covered himself with a piece of a foul, ragged cloth around his waist to his knees. He was ready to wreak havoc.

The Jackal had the head of a jackal and a body of a lean hulky man. He was very tall but not gigantic. Like the mysterious murderer, he had shadowy pigmentation, but it was not just on his face — it was his jackal head that was black. The rest of his body was pallid. He carried a pair of trench knives and two very large machetes strapped across his back. He wore a short black shenti and was barefoot – he had hocks. He was very lean, unlike the mass murderer's CrossFit and heavy lifting physique, he was like only a product of CrossFit.

Yoddha was of fair height, he was a brown skin Indian (the kind we don't see star on Bollywood). He had long black hair that reached his shoulders. He had a bit of hair on his chin. His eyes were empty, but you could see his eyeballs when his lids closed. He looked like he was in his late 20's, as that was the year he'd stopped ageing. Yoddha wore a silver cloak, the cloak always opened and spread out like wings when he engaged in combat – as a sign of warning to the opponent – rather to the people who'd commit crimes. There were constantly moving, shapeless, shadowy objects in a black muss inside the cloak. Only his hands from his wrists and his feet from his ankles were visible, apart from his face and neck. The rest of his body was buried in the shadowy muss underneath his cloak and clothes.

Bullpit was 6 foot and buff, 2 feet below Stomper. He had a body and build of an obsessed human bodybuilder, but his head was a pitbull's, and it fit nicely and did not compromise or make him look disfigured, most of that could be thanked by the mountains on either side of his neck. His humungous hands look like what I imagine muscular paws would look like, if they also had opposable thumbs. He was unrealistically muscular. He wore a black long sleeve compression shirt that outlined every single bulging muscle on his torso and arms, and a pair of brown shorts. His oddly shaped sports shoes were tailored for him, since his large feet were a combination of a paw and a human foot. If you fear pitbulls, he was scary, the muscles and height complemented each other to make him even scarier, but he was an altruistic soul, the nicest among them all, he had a strict moral code.

Amanirenas had short hair that was messy down her face, her hair was glistening blue like oil was poured over it. She was dark-skinned, the hair and her skin made her shiny magenta eyes glimmer. She was petite. Her wings were odd, they were gold and looked like a cape. She wore a high collar sleeveless white tight jumpsuit that seemed to also form shoes.

She had a diagonal scar across her nose to her right cheek, another one down her forehead that almost took out her eye, and a vertical one on the side of her face, she was heavily scarred throughout her entire body — some scars would make one question how she did not bleed to death, she was beautiful, with pretty eyes that lacked life. She was a muscular, fierce warrior.

They all watched the film, appalled by this being's sadistic actions. The middle finger part concluded their impression of this being, he was a psychopath who played with life. Bullpit said, "When you called for us and told us what had happened, I grasped the scale of this event, but seeing that this murderer slaughtered an entire population whilst having the time of his life firsthand... it fills me with rage."

"Why would someone do something like this?" Amanirenas asked with sadness. Stomper raised his voice. "It doesn't matter! We find him and we kill him!"

Athanasy cleared her throat, she looked at them with utter disappointment, they'd missed the most cardinal point, they did not ask the question they should have asked first; *'Where did he get his powers?'*. She looked at The Jackal. "Notice anything similar about him?" They all looked at The Jackal.

"Yes, the other half of my power." He answered.

Yoddha inquired, "What are you two talking about?"

The Jackal told them, "When Anathema bestowed his powers upon us, Athanasy found that my powers were halved. We concluded that perhaps they were just crude, that I could fill the other half by honing my abilities, training tirelessly until they finally bloomed to their fullest. Eventually, they did, but it would appear the other half that I had missed went to someone else."

Stomper interjected, "That is impossible. Anathema does not make mistakes."

"Then how do you explain this new being's powers? We are the only humans with such power from the only being that has the power to grant such powers, and we are the only ones with access to it. And it makes sense, the weapons, the speed, the darkness, those are the same powers The Jackal has." Amanirenas countered. The others began wondering if their powers had also been halved and shared without their knowledge, but Athanasy assured them that The Jackal was the only one with this mishap, she had an eye for such things, always have, she was a powerful psychic before Anathema granted them these powers.

Yoddha turned to Athanasy, since she knew a lot and did not think to inform them of this sooner, they could have gone out to hunt for this being and retrieve The Jackal's lost powers. He asked her, "What do you suggest we do?"

Before she could answer, Bullpit butted in with his righteous anger, "We find him and bring him to justice before he strikes again!"

Athanasy was offended that Bullpit talked over before she could answer, so she asked him with a stern tone, "And how are you going to find him?"

But Bullpit was a dog, so he knew he would say he was going to go to the scene and sniff out his scent then track him, but his insolence pushed Athanasy to tamper with his mind, so he just choked on his words and stammered. Stomper and Yoddha were aware of what Athanasy had done, Amanirenas just assumed Bullpit was stupid for not giving the most obvious answer.

"Now," she calmed herself, "since it is a piece of The Jackal's power, he will go to the city and sniff out his scent, then he will go out to hunt him and bring him to us. Alive." When Athanasy mentioned sniffing out the being's scent, the haze over Bullpit's brain cleared out and the idea came to him, but it was too late.

"Why must he be alive?" Amanirenas kindly asked. Athanasy told them she could figure out a way to retract The Jackal's power, and that she wanted to play with that murderer's soul, she said so with a sinister look on her face.

Stomper reiterated, "Anathema does not make mistakes. He is well above such things."

Bullpit countered, "Yet there lingers an evil with powers like ours, using them to harm others. If he does not make mistakes then he intentionally sabotaged us." Stomper could not stand for such blasphemy. He stood up from his chair, he leaned against the table and glowered at Bullpit. "You dare spew such profanity about Anathema?" Bullpit glowered back at Stomper, he was not scared of him.

"You're both right," Yoddha cryptically said. They turned to look at him, Athanasy was intrigued to hear what he would say. He continued, "Anathema does not make mistakes, but he also intentionally gave that evil the other half. We just need to find out why," now their eyes shifted to Athanasy. She quickly understood what they were alluding.

She utterly refused. "Summoning Anathema is a huge risk, we are not going to do that. It is too much of a price to pay for a single mad person. Out of the question! The Jackal finds him and brings him back here, then everything goes back to normal."

She was apprehensive of the idea, Anathema did not like to be summoned, he demanded a lot when summoned and he was unpredictable in his actions. There was also those tumultuous whispers of his that took residence in one's mind for days. They conceded, they cast out the idea of summoning him. Stomper sat down, but he kept staring at Bullpit, Bullpit did not stare back, he knew he could not defeat Stomper, but he would not let him treat him like he was his master. He was determined to fight, if he were to die fighting for what he believed in, then so be it.

Athanasy filled The Jackal in on the coordinates of the city and asked him to be cautious, when he asked why, she responded and advised him, "Although I infer that this copycat is of smaller stature and is a lot younger than you and lacks the precision and might you have, he still managed to slaughter an entire population and burn an entire city in a matter of minutes. He has no qualms in his actions, that makes him dangerous. If he can commit such horrendous acts whilst being frivolous, he has no conscience."

The Jackal was actually excited to meet this being, he had not had a challenge in a while. The last time he used all of his power on another being was shortly after Anathema granted them their powers. He was confident, he reminded Athanasy that he had served in the military for years and was one of the best in hand-to-hand combat. He added, "Even without these powers, my victory is guaranteed. He is sloppy, an amateur. I have experience. I will have him here before 24 hours lapses." then he headed out.

Amanirenas wanted to know their roles now that The Jackal would handle this matter. Athanasy grinned and jovially told her, "Our role is to go outside and have a joyous time with our people."

CHAPTER 3
ANTEBELLUM

In the summer of 2008, under the beautiful ocean sky and the refreshing warmth of the sun. Preence is awed by the beach house as his father's white Eldorado Biarritz Cadillac slows down into the garage of the beach house they'd rented for the summer. There weren't many trees around, so it was easy for Preence to find a favorite tree for shade. The Ekebergia Capensis tree beside the house was going to be his for the summer. He had a picture book he wanted to read for the holidays.

Preence Pygmy was 7 years old at the time, he was wearing an orange shirt with a picture of a tropical beach on the front, and a pair of black drawstring shorts with sandals. Preence's name with two e's came from his parents' childhood superhero inspiration, and the surname of his father's ancestry. His mom always called him her young prince, he loved being called her young prince. He was relatively short, for someone his age, but both his parents were 5 feet tall, so it wouldn't be a surprise if he inherits their height, especially his dad's from the Pygmy height trait. He seemed to have already been decided for on his height.

He had done a box braids hairstyle, but with dreads. He had indigo dreads curtaining halfway down his face and around his head. It was as if a spider were lolling its abnormally numerous legs.

He'd always try to group his dreads to the left side of his face to cover his black eye birthmark — his Nevus of Ota, but only at school and other places where his parents don't notice him. There had been irritable short incidents where people thought he was being abused at home or bullied at school. It took his teachers some time to accept that it was nothing but a birthmark, a bane to his face, and not a result of abuse. Black eyes disappear over time, but his hadn't disappeared since he was 4 years old, it was odd, that he'd have a birthmark at the age of 4 and not from birth, but it was normal.

The contemporary beach house had a view of the ocean to die for, Preence grabbed his backpack and ran into the house while his parents brought in their luggage and his. His mom asked him as he ran past his dad, "Please, my young prince, you don't know this house, you might hit something and injure yourself. Slow down, okay?" He said yes as he ran up the stairs.

His mother, Brenda Pygmy (her mother named her Brenda because her favorite musician was Brenda Fassie), had a perm. She was beautiful, she loved wearing big gaudy earrings. Brenda could speak half of the other tribes' languages — she spoke many languages, not just South African languages. Her mother had moved from South Africa a few years before she had her, and moved back to South Africa not more than 5 years after Brenda was born, her parents had fought and separated, and her mother's family wanted her back in South Africa. Brenda's father's pedigree was a mystery, especially since the child's tribe is determined by the father's.

She wore the same orange shirt with the tropical beach that Preence wore, and a pair of white short leggings and sandals. She was sporty, and loved showing off her calves and toned legs. Preence thought she was the coolest mom in the world. His father, Jabari Pygmy, carried in Brenda's luggage. He had albinism, that made him lighter than both his wife and child. He was of Pygmy descent, his great grandfather never really got to trace their specific surname, so he started using Pygmy as a last name —as belonging to their very own tribe. Jabari was chubby, and very hairy, but Brenda liked him hairy. His hairline was receding, but he never shaved off his hair, he didn't want to give in. He was 43 years old, and Brenda was 35 years old.

Preence loved their love story, of how they met at ComiCon (Brenda claimed she only attended the event purely out of peer pressure) and how a year later, Preence was born. Jabari wore a Hawaiian t-shirt and very colorful swim shorts. He had a thick moustache, and weary eyes, the kind of eyes that made it hard to tell if he was happy or bored, but his smile compensated for that.

He kissed his wife and told her, "Darling, let him be. He won't stop, he's too excited. He has seen the house last night, he knows his room," Brenda laughed. "I didn't know that."

Preence was relieved when he found a TV in his bedroom, he threw his backpack on the bed and checked the time on his watch, it was almost 4 pm. He had a show he was obsessed with called *Odd City*, it started in 1990, it was essentially a documentary mostly about ravaging monster who kidnap and feast upon humans and try to take over the city. But the scientists of Odd City manage to find a way to give the cops of the city mods, augmentations, and other genetic engineering programs to stop the city from falling against the ever-prowling monsters. The show was debunked and canceled because it claimed the events were based on true stories, but conspiracy theorists clung onto it. Preence was not a conspiracy theorist, he was just an avid lover of the show. He loved the show so much that it inspired him to want to be a cop when he grows up, maybe a cop version of the hero Preence that his parents loved so much that they named him after him.

The show used to air at 4 pm from Monday to Friday. After it was canceled, he was devastated, his parents had to trawl and find the show's CDs and buy them for him. All the way from the first season to the fourth, each season had 30 episodes. Since then, Preence played the CDs every weekday at 4 pm so he feels like the show was still on. He had become too attached to it, he'd watched all the 4 seasons twice, his parents didn't think much of this obsession. It was transient, he would get over it when he's older. How long can one watch the same thing over and over again and not outgrow it? Well, they did name him after a fictional character who was mentioned a few times in the Odd City show, he was believed to be an urban legend in Odd City. Seemed the parents never got over their love for their favorite animated series hero.

Later that night. Preence was sitting between his parents, watching *Shrek The Halls*. It was late, they never let him stay up past his bedtime, but schools were closed, and would reopen the following year. The big bowl filled with popcorn was on Preence's laps, since he was the one in the middle. They'd opened their doors and turned on the AC, so that Jabari doesn't take off his t-shirt and pants. He was very free and not ashamed to show his body. Though, he used to walk around shirtless back home, it didn't bother anyone. Only walking in his underpants did.

After the movie ended, the 2006 *Slither* movie was queued next, Preence's dad loved horror movies so much. Preence's mother snatched the remote and changed the channel to the next random channel, she told him, "You know we can't let my young prince watch scary movies, he will have nightmares." Preence's parents were strict of what they allowed him to be exposed to, they have been since 2 years ago when his dad fell asleep on the sofa while watching cartoons with him, he had forgotten that he had set a horror movie for later that night, he was woken by Preence's screams, he was watching the movie and it terrified him. He couldn't sleep alone for four nights.

What Brenda and Jabari didn't know was that after that traumatic period, he stopped watching the censored version of Odd City, he saw the gory, alleged actual murder scenes, the actual unedited footages of the creatures in the dark, but those episodes were mostly comprised of interviews.

Preence shrunk, and told them, "It's okay, I am going to sleep, anyway. I'm tired." Jabari asserted, "Yes! You should sleep, you need to rest. We are going to swim in the ocean tomorrow," Brenda could not find a reason to keep the movie away, she handed Jabari back the remote. Preence handed her the empty bowl as they both got up, she kissed him on the forehead and told him good night, his father also told him good night. As Brenda took the bowl to the kitchen, Preence ran up the stairs, Brenda remembered something, she shouted, "Don't forget to brush your teeth."

"I'm going to brush them right now, Mom." his voice disappeared. She went on to close all the doors and turn up the weak AC, then, she sat next to Jabari to watch the movie, she was not an enthusiast of horror, but he told her there was comedy in the movie, so she was interested. They snuggled up.

After Preence brushed his teeth, he went straight to his bedroom, catching a glimpse of the movie downstairs, he closed his bedroom door, changed into his pajamas, and laid on his bed. He loved how the moonlight shined in his bedroom. He couldn't sleep, he only said so so the night doesn't end because of him, if his parents hear the TV in his bedroom on, they would come up, so he could not watch TV. He considered watching it on mute, but, he wouldn't enjoy it. So, what to do in the meantime?

He grabbed his backpack and pulled out his Panasonic portable CD player, he was hooked on classic '90's music, especially the ballads. He thought it would be better if he listened to music while lying on the carpet inside the direct moonlight. He opened his windows, and then laid on the carpet, he could see the moon, it was a full moon, and it was, as always, beautiful and stimulating. He clicked play and relaxed with his eyes on the moon. It felt like the moon's light and the breeze from outside were bathing him, he never wanted to move from that spot. He smiled pleasantly at the moon.

He blinked, and, there was suddenly a small cat on the windowsill, it startled him, but he covered his mouth before his scream could get out. He took off his earphones and sat up while it licked its paw. He got a better look at it, it wasn't just a cat, it was a lynx kit. "What's a lynx doing at the beach?" He asked it, of course it wouldn't answer. He'd hoped this would be like in Odd City. He answered himself, "Must belong to one of the people on the beach,"

It hopped down to the carpet, and brushed itself against his arm, it seemed domesticated. It had a collar with a heart shape dangling, it read 'Felidae'.

"Felidae?" He tested, it looked up at him. He was impressed, but unfortunately he had not the means to take it in, his parents wouldn't allow it, and the owner will be distraught when they wake up and find their lynx missing. He petted it, it purred, he sighed and told it, "I'm sorry, Felidae," it looked up at him again, "but I can't take you. I have to return you to your owner, they must be worried sick about you."

He gently got up, and peeked out the window. Lynxes were known to be nocturnal, so Felidae could find its way back home, but he couldn't take it out there. The moonlight did its best, but it was still too dark for him.

He picked Felidae up and cradled him, her, oh, it was a 'her'. He asked her, "Please, show me the way to your owner, I'll take you to them." Felidae gnarled at him to continue petting her, but her gnarl was adorable. Preence chuckled and resumed petting her. Well, she had no intention of leaving. He sat down with his legs crossed with her nestled on his legs.

"There's milk in the fridge, but we don't have cat food. If I tell Mom and Dad, they would freak out. So, I'll take you to the nearby houses tomorrow, I'll return you to your owner. Or, if they call our house looking for you, I'll tell Mom and Dad and show you to them. Deal?" She purred. He tittered, "Deal."

CHAPTER 4
PEPA

Morning came, Preence's neck and back were a bit achy, because he had slept on the floor leaning against the foot of his bed petting Felidae. When he woke up, Felidae was gone. He panicked, he called for her. She reacts every time her name is uttered, so she should come out, but this time, there was no response or reaction. She was gone. He ransacked his bedroom trying to find her.

The door opened, his mother said good morning, and was mid asking him how he slept, but the messy bedroom halted her, she was befuddled, she asked him, "My young prince, what happened to your bedroom?" She entered as he stammered, she saw the open windows, now she was twice as confused. She was wearing a white slipdress, without shoes, she had her straw hat in her hands. She sternly demanded, "Tlhalosa!"

He dropped down on the pile of clothes and explained, "A small lynx jumped into my room last night while I was listening to music. Now, I can't find her. I didn't want to tell you or Dad because you would've taken her away," Brenda walked to him and crouched in front of him, she asked softly, "To the owner, yes. If you lost your pet, wouldn't you want it to be returned to you?" He nodded, he felt bad. He said softly, "I was going to return her myself, today..."

She put on her hat and put out her hands for his, he placed his hands on top of hers, she smiled and told him, "We are going to the beach today, you can "investigate" there. You can try to find out if the owner has his or her pet back." He loved that idea, he was instantly ecstatic, he hugged her and thanked her. She told him, "On one condition, you do not wander off." He agreed to the condition. Brenda clapped her hands and rushed; "Now, get up. Go get ready, I'll tidy up your room." Preence's soft voice squealed with excitement. "Thanks, Mom."

At the beach, Preence was wearing swimming trunks and a striped undershirt, his parents laid on their lounge chairs under their beach umbrellas, his father had fallen asleep with his sunglasses on, while his mother tried to read a novel while glancing up every now and then making sure he doesn't wander off too far. Jabari was shirtless with nothing but a pair of shorts, while Brenda wore a bikini, she would later swim with her son, she could not let him swim alone. There weren't many people at the beach, just a fair amount. Preence kept looking around with investigative eyes, trying to spot a cat person, someone who would likely be the owner of the lynx, or hoping to see the lynx wandering around or nestled on her owner's arms.

He spotted an elderly, chubby woman basking on her beach towel applying suntan lotion on her body. She wore a one-piece bathing suit. She had gray hair, and she looked mean. She turned and caught Preence studying her, he panicked, but she smiled and waved at him, now, now she looked like the kindest person on Earth. He waved back with a grin and was compelled to go over to her.

Brenda furrowed at him, she wondered where he was heading, she searched in the sparse crowd, she spotted the elderly woman waving at him. She worried that he might be bothering the poor woman, but then her worries quickly allayed when she saw her smiling and beckoning him. Brenda herself would presume she was the owner of the lynx kit, so she returned her attention to the novel. She couldn't help but glance one last time as her young prince and the woman exchanged greetings.

"My name's Preence — with two e's. I would like to ask you a few questions, Mrs...?"

The woman was amused, she played along. "Please, drop the Mrs., call me Helen."

"Aunt Helen, I'm sorry, but my parents don't allow me to call an adult by their name. Can I call you Aunt Helen?"

Helen laughed, and said yes, he was so adorable. She played along. He asked, "Aunt Helen, I noticed you don't have your kit with you today, do you have a kit sitter with her at your house?" Helen was confused. "A kit? I'm sorry, Detective Prince with two e's, but I have no idea what you're talking about,"

He was now uncertain. "I'm talking about Felidae, the lynx?" Maybe he jumped the gun, Helen really did not own a cat, he apologized for assuming she did. She replied casually, "Oh it's okay, Detective, I do have three cats, but not a lynx. However, I know someone who owns a lynx kit..." Preence's hopeful spark lit up, he asked ecstatically, "Who is it?"

Helen pointed behind him, as he turned, she said, "That young lady over there, Pepa, she owns a lynx. Her mother and I know each other, her mother's a zoologist." Preence saw her, he had the same happy feeling he had when he first watched Odd City. He thought he thanked Helen as his wobbly legs carried him to Felidae's owner, he felt like he was going to sweat, or was already sweating. He could always converse openly with adults, but he struggled with other kids.

Pepa, the girl who owned Felidae, was one of the lifeguards, but she was only allowed to rescue younger people with less mass, the older ones were rescued by the older lifeguards. It made sense, she was 10 years old. She wore a lifeguard hoodie and shorts, her towel was beside her, there was a red cap on her lifeguard chair. She had a whistle around her neck, and binoculars, she was so focused on her duty. She did not wear her on-duty cap because it wouldn't fit, her two ponytails held her very long hair on either side of her head. She was skinny, her skin color was honey.

Preence did not see Felidae anywhere. He trudged to Pepa as he tried to gather his dreads to hide his Nevus of Ota birthmark. He stammered 'hi' from beside the chair, Pepa lowered her binoculars and looked down at him. Her irises were sparkling green. She was Egyptian. She paused briefly when she saw him, then asked, "How can I help you?"

She was nice. Preence mumbled, she did not hear him, so she asked him to repeat what he said. An older lifeguard, Sbu, came and told Pepa it was his turn to be on duty, Pepa told him as she descended from the stairs, "Please, Sbu, look out for the kids on the northern east side, they don't have proper supervision."

Sbu peered for them with his binoculars, there were 4 kids, barely as young as Preence, playing in the water, their mother was laying on a beach towel, basking in the sun. Sbu kept his eyes on her for a while, and said lewdly, "Yeah, I don't mind watching *her* for a while," Pepa heaved and said, "Eww, just, please make sure the kids remain okay." Sbu picked up the cap from the chair and told her he would, he was known for being lascivious. He flexed a lot, and had a reputation with the women there, especially ones with kids. He had a thing for every milf he'd set his eyes upon. Hopefully he doesn't try to shoot his shot with Brenda.

Now, Pepa tended to Preence, she put her hands on her hips and asked, "What did you say your name was again?"

"Pr-Preence—two e's," he stammered, Pepa assumed he was one of the kids with speech impediments who stuttered, so she was patient and nicer. He might take a while before he tells her what he wanted. She asked him again, "How can I help you, Preence?" He tried to respond, but his throat suddenly felt dry. Pepa chuckled and offered him some water. She started walking, he followed. He didn't know where she was going or why he was following her.

There was a cooler box filled with water bottles reserved for lifeguards near the changing rooms, she took out a bottle of water for him and asked him to wait for her. "I'm done for the day, I'm going to change out of my uniform, then hopefully you'll be in a better condition to communicate after drinking some water, then you can tell me what's wrong, okay?" He nodded.

He waited for her on a crate as he guzzled the water, he didn't know why he couldn't talk properly around her, maybe she was magical. Yes! Like in Odd City, they had done an episode about mermaids of unfathomable beauty, they'd lure men to the ocean and then devour them. He forgot he could not talk to any of his peers. Was she really in the changing room getting out of her uniform or was she devising on how to get him aloof and then kill him? He shook his head, this is what his parents warned him about, watching conspiracy theories documentaries makes one paranoid and detached. He noticed he hadn't done a good job hiding his birthmark, and grunted at himself.

He saw her emerge from the changing rooms wearing a one-piece bathing suit and pink shorts, she was barefoot, but so was he. He felt a lot better, maybe he really needed water. She stopped in front of him, handed him a pair of shorts she got from the lost & found, and asked caringly, "You feeling better?" He said yes, he could talk perfectly, now. Well, water doesn't free you from a mermaid's spell, and your spell binder wouldn't give you the antidote for a spell she cast on you. He felt silly for thinking she was a mermaid.

He told her, "I heard you own a lynx, Felidae? She jumped into my room last night, I just wanna let you know she was okay, and, I just wanna know if she's okay now. If you're okay, you must've been worried."

She breathed a sigh of relief, and told him, "Thank goodness, I was worried that aliens might've kidnapped her and are now impersonating her," saying it out loud made her feel embarrassed, she cringed and said awkwardly, "I'm sorry, that sounds crazy," she seemed intensely embarrassed, that made him wonder if she cared so much about what strangers think of her. He spontaneously countered, "Crazy? I thought you were a mermaid with a spell over me that made me stammer." He quickly cringed, why did he say that?

She laughed, she had a quirky laugh, her older sister had said if she were older and continued to laugh like that, people would say it was not "lady-like".

"Maybe we're both crazy." He laughed, too. She offered, "Wanna visit Felidae? I'm sure she'd love to see you,"

"Are you kidding? Of course I do. She kept trying to scare me into petting her, but she was too cute."

"Really? She only lets me or my mom pet her, she's very feisty. She never lets anyone get close to her."

"Guess I'm special." Preence said bashfully. Pepa giggled. They walked to the beach houses, farther from Preence's parents', he had not forgotten his promise to his mother that he wouldn't wander off, his investigation had taken him someplace else, if his mother panics and starts thinking he's missing, he hoped Aunt Helen would ease her worries.

The area to Pepa's home was surrounded by trees, unlike the houses for rent that had not more than a single tree, some two at most. "So, you live here, you're not on vacation?" He asked her, her house was big, she opened the gate, her home had a picket fence, and she led him to the door. Preence had never been in a house as spacious as Pepa's, and he could not hide his awe.

There was an older girl in the house, Pepa's older sister, Cleopatra (a traditional name), she was sitting in the living room with Felidae lying beside her on the couch, she had long hair, too, and had darker complexion. She seemed reserved, and she was kind and bubbly. She was watching a reality show, Pepa teased her for watching that show too much, she deflected by telling her she also watched Odd City too much, then they broke out in laughter.

Pepa and Preence then headed out, Preence heard Cleopatra mention Odd City, so he brought it up on their way to his house. Pepa said she literally could not stop watching Odd City, she could not let herself forget about it as soon as it was canceled. Felidae was behaving, she did not scratch Preence. Pepa asked him, "What's the scariest episode for you?"

"Oh, the scariest episode? For me, I think it's season 3 episode 13."

"*The Kgwenyape*, the one where the humungous snake hid in the sky during a massive tornado, actually it was the one that caused the storm, right? It's my number 2 scariest. It's amazing how the Odd City Police managed to stop it."

"What's your number 1?"

"*The Sleep Paralysis Hag*, season 2 episode 5,"

"Oh, that one gave me nightmares. She just sits on your chest while you sleep, it scares you more because she wakes you up and you can see her gawking down at you while she grins. Her old, yellow, missing teeth, feeling her toenails prodding your chest. Sometimes her top half just wanders around your house, breaking things while her lower part keeps you paralyzed—"

"Preence! Please! That episode still scares me today," Pepa lamented. There was a brief aggressive wind, but fortunately, without the dust. Felidae cowered in Preence's arms, so he covered her and hunched over her. Pepa, on the other hand, loved the wind, she spread her arms and closed her eyes. She looked so tranquil.

CHAPTER 5
THE SKY CAN BLEED LEECHES

Pepa loved cars, especially the popular ones from the '80's. Seeing Preence's dad's Cadillac blew her away. When Preence was closing the garage door, he saw something perched on top of one of her ponytails. She could not get enough of touching the Cadillac, she was rather too fond of it, Preence wondered if it was her dream car. The garage door plunking startled Felidae, she hopped off his arm and disappeared somewhere in the garage.

Preence walked up to Pepa, and picked off something from her hair, something that had stuck to her hair when the wind blew. They both gasped at it, for different reasons, Preence held it between him and her, it was a pink feather. There were flamingos on the beach, so the excitement of finding feathers had grown hackneyed for Pepa.

"Season 1, episode 24; *Messages From The Angels*." Preence said to her with excitement in his tone. She stuck out her tongue lackadaisically and said, "Yawn. I want to watch season 4, it's the best season. I don't even remember what color the feathers represented, the first season is mostly just old farts sharing information, barely any footages or uncovering secrets of the deep. It always felt like I was in school — a school for old people."

Preence laughed. "A school for old people? Is it real?" He closed his hand with the pink feather in there, and held on to it. Pepa asked him shyly, "Why are you keeping it?" She was actually happy he did not throw it away. He smiled affectionately at the feather, and told her, "After we watch season 4, I'm going to rewatch season 1's episode 24 to remember what this means." She covered his hand with both her hands, and looked at him with a special glint in her green eyes, she said, "I won't check to remember what it means, I'll wait for you to tell me," Preence blushed, too.

Felidae jumped from one of the shelves, she did not knock over any boxes. She stood in front of the fire-rated door. Preence and Pepa were already becoming close, like most Odd City fans. If you find someone as weird as you or someone who likes the same hated show as you, a friendship doesn't take long to build.

In his bedroom, Pepa scooted to his bed as soon as she got a good look at the TV angle, she sat facing right at it, and waited for him. He laughed, placed the feather in the drawer, and hurried to the DVD, he searched for the remote, around the DVD behind the TV, he wondered where he'd put it. He never forgets or misplace his stuff. Felidae had walked in after Pepa, she walked past them and jumped to the windowsill.

"You looking for this?" Pepa asked, she had the remote in her hand, she handed it to him, he thanked her and said with relief, "I was scared, I thought I'd lost it," Pepa laughed and said spontaneously, "Then, you need a weird friend to make sure you don't lose anything else again," she quickly withdrew and smiled. Preence smiled, too.

A list of folders titled 'Odd_City_season_1' to season 4 appeared on the screen, Preence scrolled down to season 4, opened the folder, and asked her, "Re lebelle e feng?" She pointed at the first episode and said jovially, "All of them, from the first episode." Then she giggled. He sat next to her. From the first episode, Preence had realized that he was wrong when he thought the best feeling of watching Odd City was with his parents, the feeling magnified when he watched it with Pepa, a fellow Odd City geek. They were both so young and innocent, free from trauma. For the time being.

During the fifth episode credits, Preence was about to play the sixth episode, but Pepa asked him not to skip the credits, he asked her why, she told him, "To get a chance to talk. What influence has Odd City had in your life, or your view of the world?"

He sat back, well, that was a question he'd never thought about or anticipated ever being asked. For a 7-year-old, watching a creepy documentary that was meant for people from 18 years and older (without the censors), only one response came to mind. He said, "I want to be a cop, like the ones in Odd City."

"That much of an influence, huh?" She was deeply impressed. He loved her reaction so much he had his nose up with a big grin. She clapped her hands and said, "You, Preence, are a true Odd City geek, like me, which is a good thing. Normal is like season 1 of Odd City,"

"The farts?" He asked, she popped her quirky laugh and said yes. The farts. He wanted to thank her for being the first and only person who has never asked him about his black eye birthmark or stare at it funny, or even stare at it at all, but if he mentions it, then he makes the whole thing weird and he would become the one highlighting his birthmark.

She said, suddenly, "I like season 4 because it's the one that fits the synopsis of the entire show best," Preence did not know what a synopsis was, "It has a lot of animals, creatures, beasts, all that. My mom's a zoologist, but she moved to Europe, I live here in South Africa with my sister and my dad. My grandparents are originally from Egypt. My mom got me Felidae as a birthday gift this year. She sends me videos of her and the animals there every chance she gets. I want to be like her, to be a zoologist, but for mystical creatures, you know..." she laughed at herself. "I know, it's an impossible dream, it's... crazy. My sister says I'll grow up someday and it will wear off, I really wish I could find Odd City,"

He said to her, "It is a crazy dream, but not an impossible one, crazy is fun, and crazy is Odd City. I can help you find Odd City." Pepa thanked him. The credits ended, he had to play the next episode as they didn't automatically play one after the other.

Later that night, before Preence went to sleep, after he'd told Brenda of how wonderful his day was with Pepa, how cool Pepa was, and that she was the owner of Felidae, he asked Brenda if he could use her BlackBerry to chat with Pepa. Brenda was just happy to see him so happy, so she agreed, but she was eager to see this girl and Felidae.

Preence took some time to get a hang of the keyboard, then he sent Pepa a text message saying that he had found out what the pink feather meant, it signified love. Their love was the friendship kind, because they were too young for the other kind of love, except Pepa believed she might have felt something like that kind of love toward Preence, but that was because of the movies above her age restrictions that she watched a lot. He was weird, like her. She cherished him, not just as her newest best friend, but also as Felidae's best friend.

He spent the festive season with his new best friends, Pepa and Felidae, around. His parents still thought Pepa was too old to hang out with him, but they were really close, and they were both obsessed with Odd City, and honestly, they were just kids, so, why be the unnecessary villain? Pepa showed Preence the videos her mother had sent her, the animals were adorable, and they really loved her mother. The two spent the summer days in the beach, swimming, watching Odd City, playing make-believe games where they imagined the world around them was Odd City, they also read the picture book Preence had under the Ekebergia Capensis tree in the shade on top of a beach towel. Pepa taught him a lot of new words and defined some from the story that he didn't understand, she was so smart.

During the night of the 31st of December, everyone gathered at the beach to countdown and light some fireworks, Pepa and Preence were extremely happy and wholly into the festive spirit, but January 2009 meant going back to school and that was disappointing, because he did not live there, she did, he would have to leave.

Before the countdown began, she had snuck away with him to her house, Cleopatra was having a party, their father was barely around, so Cleopatra did everything she wanted. There was smoking and drinking at the party, the smell of alcohol made Preence gag as they snuck past the older kids. Pepa took him to the roof of her house, said they'd get the best view of the fireworks, Preence was unsteady and trembling on the roof, but Pepa held his hand, and promised him she would not let him fall. He trusted her. His parents had left for at a braai near the beach to watch fireworks with their new friends, including Aunt Helen.

"I hate that we have to go back to school," She sulked. He felt the same way, but he wholeheartedly believed he could convince his parents to visit again during the holidays. He wanted to cry, she was on the brink of crying, he needed to be a big boy for the moment and not cry. He surprised her with the pink feather, it was inside a marble, like a snow globe, it was beautiful. He told her as she held it and was astonished by it, "I asked my parents to make it like that, I found it on the morning of Christmas, as a gift."

"I thought you'd forgotten about this, this is so sweet," she said with her eyes glued to the marble. He murmured with a red face ready to burst, "I would never forget..."

"Let's make a promise," she said with an upbeat tone, she enclosed her hand with the feather-marble inside, he was listening, and in his head he already agreed to whatever she'd say.

She said, "You hold on to this, you give it to me when you come visit again. I'll raise Felidae, and we'll wait for you. She will be so big when you visit again. Promise you'll come back?" the countdown had begun, now nearing zero. He said, "I promise." Then, she suddenly kissed him on the cheek as the clock reached zero and the older kids in the house cheered and the fireworks claimed the sky.

For the next months of 2009, Preence used his mother's phone constantly to keep in touch with Pepa. They spoke for hours on end, Brenda had (even though Jabari protested against) eavesdropped on their phone calls to hear what they talked about for so long, it was usually about how their days were, describing even every bit of unnecessary detail, but on every call, Pepa mentioned Felidae. Preence's performance at school actually went from good to excellent, Pepa was a positive influence on him. Brenda never thought her young prince's first best friends would be a girl and a lynx kit.

December 2009.

One would have expected their friendship to wane over time, that they would start talking less and end up not talking any more, but, their friendship was ever bright. That moment when Preence stood outside the beach house, Pepa at the gate with Felidae, who had grown so big that she was scary to strangers, Preence had shaved his hair and grown a few inches tall, he had the feather-marble in his hand, Pepa's hairstyle was the same, and she was a lot taller than when Preence last saw her. At that beautiful moment before they rush to each other and embrace each other, the sky turned black. The sky leeches were upon the people of Earth.

There were enormous leeches in the sky, their Y-shaped mouths opened and started flooding the earth with leeches. It was abrupt, no warning, one moment the sky is clear, the next, there were hundreds of giant leeches.

Felidae bared her teeth and gnarled at the leeches, but Pepa froze, the sky, this event reminded her of the episode in Odd City of the giant snake in the sky causing storms. Preence rushed to her, and pulled her inside the house, just in time to grab Felidae's leash before she could run off. One knows Felidae would have been a danger to the people trying to survive as she was spooked. Preence had petted her to calm her down before running into the house for shelter.

His parents called Pepa's house to let them know of her whereabouts, and by them, I mean Cleopatra. Their dad was practically a memory that became real for a day or two then faded. The leeches weren't much of a threat, unless their rain pours on you. Those who were fortunate enough to find shelter on time had to watch those who weren't get sucked dry by the countless leeches outside. Those things were not ordinary leeches. Preence held Pepa's hand tightly throughout the event while petting Felidae with the other.

They were in the living room, as the sky turned darker and the earth blacker with leeches. Pepa was still stuck in her frozen state, she wasn't kidding when she said episode 13 was her second scariest episode. It was Preence's number one scariest episode, and he was petrified, but he could not let her be a victim of whatever was happening. Imagine if the sleep paralysis old hag was the one who had come instead. Pepa would have died of fright.

Maybe the ones who'd died during the rain were the lucky ones. Because they did not get to see what the sky leeches could do. Minutes later, Preence opened his eyes, he saw his parents and everyone else lifting to the sky, he was outside — they were all outside. He did not know what had happened, if he had blacked out. He felt someone pulling his hand. It was Pepa, she was trying to pull him away so they could run, but there was really nowhere to run. She never let go of his hand.

All of the people in the sky above them, their skins began being sucked out from the bodies, like pulling the peel off. They screamed, Preence now froze. He saw his parents, too, even Aunt Helen, their blood was being sucked into the sky leeches' mouths. Then, he began lifting off the ground, Pepa's hand slipped from his, he slowly span uncontrollably as he was being taken to the sky. He got to see her. She was screaming his name, she was crying, she was reaching out for him to grab her hand as she also fell victim to the gravity-suspended phenomenon, she was covered in blood spatter, he hoped it wasn't Felidae's.

Preence didn't realize he'd lost the feather-marble, he had no idea where it was. He tried to swim his way to her, he thought the blood on her was hers, if he would die, he would die next to her. His skin began feeling like it was compressing his flesh, his fingers and Pepa's finally reached each other. They pulled each other in and had their momentous hug, they both shut their eyes, they were crying, the things they've just seen. Everything turned black.

The last thing Pepa and Preence saw were each other's faces.

CHAPTER 6
THE SKEWED BUILDING

The Jackal arrived at the scene at dusk, they could not place a yellow tape around the curtain wall of an entire city so they just put it at the tall gate. The city was charred to the ground, it seemed like a place that was left derelict for years, but the smell of fire still lingered strongly, and the ashes of the civilians were mixed with the ashes of the city. If you would listen closely, the wind sounded like the screams of the dead.

The scene was nearly teeming, Athanasy really went out of her way to deploy as many officers as possible from her city and another nearby city to the scene, but cautious not to leave the two cities vulnerable. Besides, the other city was nearer to the city the Sentinels of Anathema were gathered in, and Pygmy would either be suicidal, foolish, presumptuous or very powerful to attack either of these cities.

The investigators were all occupied, only the heavily armed dozen guards at the gate saw The Jackal coming, they had shot and killed three gigantic beasts that used to be crocodiles. They all wore olive green uniforms and black peaked caps despite them being from different cities – this was because they were all under the same authority.

They all took a bow and greeted The Jackal in perfect unison. There was one timid lanky man who walked toward The Jackal as the others continued with their work, he gestured a salute and began filling him in. The Jackal's nose was repressed by the strong odor in the air, so he required their aid. Something was amiss, The Jackal had a persistent feeling that something had occurred before his arrival, but that was probably his alertness scouring for any threat so he could eliminate it. Probably.

Since everything except their statues was burned down and the tallest building was destroyed, The Jackal could not pinpoint the exact location Pygmy had dwelled the longest so he could cling onto his scent, so the lanky man, who turned out to be the captain, led him to it, there was too much debris to get through as they made way to the spot. The Jackal could not wait to get Pygmy's scent and hunt him down, he had not felt such excitement in a long time.

Pygmy walked to the cracked windowpane of that old bedroom to get a better view of the sunset over the ocean, intently watching nature and admiring it in a nigh enthralled state always seemed to calm him and made him feel like he was not alone. The old beach house was a broken reminder of what used to be. Under the pending night, where he lurked, was just a darkness devoid of electricity or civilization. He wanted to visit a spot in the ruined city not too far from the town. There were trees growing from the rubbles, ivies slithering on walls, and fissures that claimed the roads to remind whoever of what had occurred, there were vast burrows that seemed infinite on the ground sparse near the beach. The only thing keeping the creatures, what had become of the animals of this world, from attacking was the many years of slaughtering and hunting for food. The creatures had begun evading his vicinity because they were aware they were his food.

He missed his parents and Pepa so very much for the past 16 years, but he knew he could never get them back, the only way for him to see them again was if he dies, which he longed for, but his grudge prohibited him from allowing himself to perish just yet. There was a period in the beginning of those early years when his mind was always plagued with suicidal thoughts, and consequently almost led to numerous suicidal attempts, but he eventually concluded that if he were to die anyway, then it should be by the hand of his enemies. He had a mission, now. It fueled his grit and made him ever industrious.

He still visited the ruined beach house some nights – this was one of those nights, he felt closer to his family and Pepa and Felidae there than any other place. He lived nearby, but that mattered not as he could, if he lived far, blink back home. He used to hydrate himself by drinking the ocean water, since he was not entirely human anymore the need for food and water did not impair him, he could go for weeks without water and food, but his exhaustive sessions required a lot of energy so he had to eat and stay hydrated.

Later on, he walked to a skewed tall office block in what remained of the city, the view he had from the city he had just destroyed had rubbed off on him, he actually stuck around for a while after murdering that man to enjoy the serene feeling that such views brought, such feelings he was used to, it was familiar with watching the sun set, the stars and the moon, the ocean waves, the waving trees. The new impression of city lights perhaps had something to do with a man-made view, he had been getting ample nature views.

As he walked up the stairs, he had heard strange fleeting sounds from the building, he figured some of the beasts had crawled into the building some time before his arrival, but he was not worried. Although he had left his weapons home and still required some rest from the mass murder, he could take them on, so he continued up the stairs. He had to jump over some gaps as some parts of the stairs were demolished. The only thing that was perceivable in the darkness on his face when he was not grinning was his graphite eyes.

Along the stairs, there was a complete blockage of cluttered debris in his way that would collapse if he tried to move them, so he settled for that floor, it was high enough. He passed a couple of "cramped office boxes" and walked to the one on the other side of the lopside, he walked to the broken windows to indulge in the amenities of the view. It was one of those glass buildings. He saw the grim dead city, but captured it in its mind, shut his eyes and imagined it was a splendor of lights, like the city he had just burned to the ground. But his view was short-lived.

He felt a sudden bashing on his back, sending him through the broken glass, but he was quick enough to grab ahold of the edge of the window and do a 180 degrees onto the window next to it, the thing that had hit him grabbed his legs and started yanking him down so they could fall together. The pull of this creature was strong enough to make him lose his grip, they both tumbled down the glass windows at least six floors down before he brought himself to a stop, the creature stopped diagonally away from him.

It was not like any of the animals that had morphed into vicious predators of the new world, it was a big, brawny creature with a body of a human. It had gold skin with no facial features, just nothingness and a ceaseless muffled screech underneath, it was a surprise that Pygmy did not hear it coming. No, it started with the screeching after it attacked him. Its groin was dangling around in the glass shards as it stood crouched poised to attack.

Precipitously, a sizzling burning crimson tongue wrapped around Pygmy's waist and yanked him back into the building. Pygmy sawed the tongue off him with his barbed wire on his vambraces as it threw him into wall after wall swinging him around ceaselessly. By the time he managed to free himself, he was against a dented wall above a broken elevator in the shaft. He examined himself, the heat of the tongue could be felt on his breastplate, but it was unaffected. The tongue suddenly appeared before him, shooting at very high-speed – aiming for his head, he ducked it and nearly slipped.

He swung his arm to grab the tongue but it was drawn back to the skulking owner. Then, as he was about to chase after the tongue, he heard clacks and felt pricks on his right bicep, when he turned to see, it was another golden naked creature, this one wore gauntlets of numerous layered claws, but Pygmy could not discern that. It had no face either. The creature was trying to sink its claws into his skin, but he had tough skin.

He reached to grab its hand, it attempted to swiftly draw back but he managed to grab it, he swung it up the shaft, it missed his face with a few claws. Thanks to his fine reflexes he had recoiled in the nick of time. He bounced off the walls of the shaft as he chased after it. His plan was to get away from that exposed wall so the sly tongue does not get him.

He managed to thrust his boots down its face and projected it even farther aloft, then continued up the shaft as he chased after it. He glanced down and saw that the muffled screeching one had entered the shaft and was rapidly crawling up to them. The creature with the claws attacked him, he dodged, redirected and blocked its seamless attacks as they jumped from wall to wall. The contact between the claws and his barbed wire caused sparks. The muffled screeching creature caught up to them, Pygmy swung around the elevator cable to dodge it, then thrusted his boot down its back, pinning it against the wall. The one with the claws swiped at his face, he ducked it and steadied his right foot down the screeching one's face. He grabbed the creature's lower back as it was still in motion and dug his fingers into its skin and catapulted it through the wall.

He focused on the one he'd pinned against the wall, he was about to kill it when something blasted through the shaft from above. It was a very tall, morbidly obese gold creature that practically blocked the entire shaft with its body, it was the creature with the tongue... tongue*s*. It had openings on both palms frothing excessively with numerous tongues sticking out loosely, the creature was also buck naked, but its numerous folds of skin hid its groin. Pygmy saw the wreckage that followed this creature, so he stomped the pinned creature on its neck, spun then kicked it down the shaft with more vigor, then he bolted out of the shaft through the hole he'd opened by catapulting the creature with the claws.

Multiple tongues wrapped around his leg and started pulling him back into the shaft. He grabbed the tongues and wrapped them around his arms and planted both his feet firmly on the floor and was able to halt himself. The wreckage dropped down along with the creature with the tongues, it was as if the creature had caused a collapse of the building into the shaft. The tongues finally tore off, Pygmy cast them onto the floor and watched them squirm, he figured to a normal human a touch of one tongue was enough to cause third degree burns. He wanted burn marks.

He was tired, he took a deep breath to try to make sense of everything. It was evident this was an attack, the Sentinels of Anathema were retaliating. This realization drew the maniacal smile on his face, his heart started pulsating. He wanted them to find him, and they did, his adrenalin was coursing through his body, it was such an exhilarating feeling.

As he was standing there grinning mischievously into space, the creature with the claws snuck up behind him to claw him. In a single skip of breath, there was a gust of wind that nearly shook the floor, blood was splattered everywhere, he had run through its body at very high speed in that short distance. He made the creature's body pop like a water balloon, but spared its head. He turned and grabbed its head with both hands as couples do before they start smooching. His body was drenched in blood. He turned it to face him and gazed into its empty face, he said jovially, "You came! You know where I live, so you bring more! Send more! Please!" then he laughed like a crazy person.

There was grumbling in the building, he crushed the head like a watermelon. He hopped back to a safer distance, an elevator catapulted angularly from the ground up, the others had thrown an elevator at him. He was amazed of the strength these creatures had, and excited. The ceiling began collapsing along with other floors above him, he continuously recoiled until he broke out of the window, he looked up and saw the elevator arching over in the sky with a wide smile.

He turned his head as if someone had wrung it and saw the screeching creature charging toward him, shattering away the windowpanes at each heavy swift step. He knew the one with the tongues would surprise him with a sneak attack, so he knew what he had to do. He blasted off forward, shooting out shards of glasses from what remained of the windows. The creature did not see him coming, it was as though he had disappeared and appeared before it, with a squelch and a sudden knot in its stomach. He had punched it in the gut, the force was enough to sink his fist into its stomach then he shoved his arm into its rib cage and crushed whatever organ he could get ahold of or whatever was going on inside that thing's body, then he placed his other hand on its back and started spinning it around at very high speed that it caused a small gust, parts of the creature's body started shooting out of the vortex piece by piece.

When Pygmy finally stopped, there weren't any more glasses left, and the only thing in his hands was... well, nothing remained. In fact, the spin had shaken off the blood that had been smeared on him. He had spotted the tongues withdrawing as he was spinning the muffled-screeching creature, the other one had wanted to attack but it saw no opening and it was aghast of what he was doing to the other creature. He let himself freefall beside the building, staring indifferently into the building floor by floor hoping to spot the creature with the tongues. It became clear to Pygmy that it was fleeing when he was four floors away from the ground. He disappeared suddenly with a grin.

CHAPTER 7
IN THE CITY

Half an hour after the attack on Pygmy, The Jackal was racing through the wilderness burning with an urge to clobber Pygmy and off his head. While on the way, he continuously fantasized of many creative and torturous methods he would use to kill Pygmy, but he was not allowed to kill him. He was the quickest on his feet in all of the Sentinels of Anathema, which was evident in Pygmy's remarkable speed, they shared the same power, after all.

He slowed down when he spotted something strange up a slope he was running toward, he could not make out what it was as he had never seen anything like it before, but he knew for a fact it was not Pygmy, he raised his velocity higher than it was before. The closer he drew to this thing, the more he could make out what it was. It finally became discernable, but The Jackal was still baffled. He did not have a clue of what it was, but it felt... it couldn't be. He gasped.

It was the creature with the tongues that was sent to kill Pygmy, it stood torpid and lifeless, with poorly done stitches all over its body, strange fluids seeped past the stitches. It had an awful smell that went right up The Jackal's nose, the smell was so intolerable that The Jackal wished to never smell anything like it ever again. He covered his nose and recoiled to a safer distance. It was definitely not a mutated animal.

He called out to it, "Who are you? How did you get here? Where did you come from?" This was odd, it was sent along with the other two to off Pygmy as reprisal, but The Jackal did not know about it, but he knew what it was – he was appalled by what it was. It just stood there dead silent, or maybe just dead. The Jackal could perceive that it was dead, but he could hear a faint heartbeat. He threatened it to raise its hands or he would attack.

Then, it slowly and laboriously began raising its loose arms, but its face, it did not have a face, just creased folds of skin.

"Now, I will ask again; how did you get here?" He asked sternly. At least it was still alive, he could get some answers out of it. If it had a mouth hidden in all that crease. It took its time before it responded, The Jackal was fuming. It replied, "Why? You believed you had killed all humans outside your cities?" A muffled voice, almost in a jest-like tone, replied from within.

The Jackal thought that was a very strange response, but he knew what that thing was talking about. He pulled out one machete, he asked again, "How did you get here?" It was correct, he did believe all humans outside the cities were dead, but the Sentinels did not kill the humans. It chuckled, then the chuckle turned into a maniacal laughter, then, slowly, the creature tipped over. When it hit the ground the stitches could not bear to hold anymore, now its fluids were leaking out everywhere and its torn skin looked like a bunch of dirty wash rags - which fueled the pervasive awful smell, but The Jackal's focus was fixed on something else.

Pygmy was standing over the creature, he was covered in the creature's unidentifiable fluids and blood, his hair was moist but still looked solid. He had been hiding inside the creature for God-knows how long, waiting for the Sentinels of Anathema to send the next wave of attack. He now only wielded his Zulu axe and his iklwa. He burped and told The Jackal as The Jackal pulled out the second machete, "Yes, that thing used to be human, long ago. You perverted so-called heroes really know how to take things to another level."

The Jackal brandished his weapons and got into a stance. "Well, since you know everything, we can't let you live. You are no better than us, you're out here deforming and making human puppets and committing mass murders, unlike you, we do not enjoy doing the things we've done."

"Someone is keeping secrets," Pygmy giggled with his fingers fidgeting in front of his lips and his shoulders jerking. The Jackal did not understand what he was implying, but he did not care at that moment.

He said with reproach, "You burned down an entire city and filmed yourself doing it, none of them deserved to die."

Pygmy stopped fidgeting and dropped his hands and narrowed his eyes, he said with a smirk, "Oh, I wasn't the one who set them on fire," The Jackal was confounded, this mass murderer kept hinting at things that piqued his curiosity. He was hinting at things that The Jackal could not ignore. The Jackal started wondering if he really had allies who helped him in the city, but the film showed none but himself, and also, he had a mutated creature of what used to be human, he must have had a lot more of these puppets assisting him. But he did say something about secrets, and The Jackal himself knew there weren't any humans left, he would smell them if there were any, so what did Pygmy mean when he said someone is keeping secrets?

Pygmy had planned to fight The Jackal, but now he had other plans, since he realized The Jackal did not know about the attack or these creatures, he could use that to his advantage, maybe pit the Sentinels of Anathema against each other, since some of them had secrets. He tilted his head and planted a final seed, "These things," he pointed at the creature on the ground, "aren't as fast as me or you, and somehow they got to me before you did. Strange, isn't it?" Then, he vanished as The Jackal lunged at him.

The Jackal could not sense or smell him anymore, he knew he did not run, that was another thing that concerned him — this being could teleport, but he couldn't, and they had the same power. Now, Pygmy's scent was masked by the creature's stench, and that smell stung The Jackal's nose, so he had no desire to use it to track Pygmy, he was now more focused on finding answers. Pygmy had gotten away. The Jackal quickly meditated on the situation then decided to return to the city to find answers.

There were two people, a man and a woman, quaint and off-putting, at a restricted floor of the tower. They were having very aggressive sex. They seemed to glitch here and there as though they were not real, but they were very real, so were the woman's piercing moans and the man's bestial grunts. Luckily for the poor ones near who would be susceptible to such noises, their room was soundproof for this sole purpose.

The man's hands gripped the woman's hips so tightly it looked as though his fingers would sink into her skin and bleed her. She had pink flushes and contusions. The woman's legs kept violently shaking, you'd think she was having a seizure if you had an angle of POV that showed solely her legs.

The man had her bent over and was pounding her, and at fleeting moments, it hurt her, but she loved it. The pain was the pleasant kind to her. She loved the 'pain and pleasure' ambivalence. She had her hands clutching the silky sheets, she was sweating profusely, she and the man both were. They climaxed at the same time, the man did not withdraw, and the woman did not mind, they had a way around that. After their ferocious session, which had lasted for hours, they laid beside each other naked on the bed with the blankets on. They did not talk to each other, they just flashed awkward smiles at each other when their eyes accidentally met then quickly averted their eyes.

The man asked her, while catching his breath, "How much time do we have left?"

The woman, panting, replied taking breaths in between her sentence, "It should wear off in an hour or two." Their interaction was not an awkward one, but it was plain to see that it was merely for sex, nothing more.

The woman got out of bed, she appeared subtly irritated, she walked to the window wall to admire the beautiful sight of the city lights. A view Pygmy wished for. She was staring blankly down at the people, the man did not seem to mind, until the woman sensed something that sent shivers down her spine. She placed both hands on the glass window, she danced her eyes around as she squinted. She was scouring for something.

The man asked her, he was concerned, "What's wrong, Athanasy?"

She did not reply, she just continued squinting down at the people, it was true people of the city never slept. The man asked again, she replied, she was annoyed, "I heard you the first time, Stomper." Then she continued peeping.

The man, apparently Stomper, got out of bed and walked up to her, he thought her worry had something to do with the mass murderer who sent them the film. Or it could be that she was standing naked where everyone in the near buildings could see her. Well, she was under a disguise and she always wore very scant clothes so she did not care if people saw her bare. She had cast a spell on both of them to temporarily make them entirely human again so that they can have sex without trashing the place and endangering the lives of the people in that tower.

Athanasy was sensing something, some*one* who stood out in the crowd. She told Stomper, "There is someone in the city, someone who feels like us. Not like the people down there,"

"Could it be him?"
"I don't know, probably."

"But that wouldn't make any sense, The Jackal would also be here. You sent him after his scent, right?"

Athanasy briefly paused, then returned her focus to her search. She reverted to her true form, Stomper was a little confounded, but of course she could skip the timer on the spell, she was the one who cast it, after all. She said with urgency, "We have an intruder. Yoddha is still in the city. I will alert him and tell him to find this person before they escape." Stomper asked her to turn him back to normal. "I will go guard the gate so they don't escape." And so, Athanasy did.

She telepathically searched for Yoddha throughout the city and called for him. Stomper burst out of the window and took a beeline to the gate, he could fly. As soon as Yoddha answered, Athanasy relayed in a succinct manner, "We have an intruder in our city! I'll guide you to him! Stomper is on his way to the gate so this person doesn't escape!" Yoddha did not waste any time, despite him wanting to ask the same question Stomper asked about The Jackal tracking the mass murderer's scent.

There were small dark particles gathering in the night sky above the city, it was practically impossible to spot them, they were emanating from Yoddha's cloak as he flew through the city following Athanasy's faltering directions to this intruder, but he was getting close, but then Athanasy was suddenly unresponsive. Yoddha halted above a crowd that was crossing the street at an intersection, he could not sense the intruder, so he was blind since Athanasy had suddenly disappeared. The crowd and the cars stopped and people took out their phones to record him and cheer for him, but Yoddha was the only one in the Sentinels of Anathema who did not like the fame, but this was good, no one was moving, it made it easier to spot the intruder if they made a run for it.

Athanasy's voice popped up suddenly in his head, he wanted to swear at her, but he just took a deep weary breath. She told him, "I had to isolate the city, so everything is shut down, no internet, nothing. So that the other cities do not see what's happening here," of course, to prevent chaos and panic, they had told the other cities that the city Pygmy had burned down was facing some issues they refused to elaborate on.

Athanasy did not peer for long, she exclaimed, "There he is! The man with the white hair!" Yoddha spotted him, he had his black mass poised to cage the man inside and forcefully push out the crowd should the man show any sign of aggression. Though, he did not have crowd control skills, he despised crowds. Athanasy felt she had seen the man before, somewhere, from a very distant, vague memory, but it slipped out of her reach and she forgot about it.

The man Athanasy had pointed out was so terrified and confused that Yoddha quickly felt bad for him. He sincerely did not look like he knew what was happening, if he were the intruder then maybe he only sneaked into the city to live the life.

"Except he is not registered in any of the cities. Hold him there, I'm on my way." Athanasy said clamantly. The poor man begged for Yoddha to let him go, he was hyperventilating. The crowd was now confused, why was Yoddha targeting this poor man. The man did not cease to beseech, he decided to ask Yoddha what he did wrong, and if this were a test. Yoddha silently stared at him with pity.

The man dropped on his knees, cast his phone on the tarmac, put his hands together and cried for Yoddha to tell him what was going on. This was quickly becoming uncomfortable for the people. They tried to stream it live, but the internet was down. Yoddha questioned him, "Who are you? Where did you come from?" The man stammered, his voice was trembling, he was sweating. He was definitely not the mass murderer, but he had no ID in any of the cities, so Yoddha could not let him go until Athanasy arrives and explains everything. He telepathically asked Athanasy how she spotted the man so quickly, but she had cut their telepathic communication. The crowd was growing, and the noise grew more and more.

The man appeared to be in his early hale 30's. His dark skin was suffused with vibrant-colored symbolic tattoos, lists of names, illustrations of particular events of wars, full-body arts of the many dragons he admired and whose characteristics he wished to emulate. His face was probably the only part of his body that was untouched. He had very long, white dreads, some hid half of his face, the rest of his locks were tied to a very long ponytail. He had a grayish stubble. He wore an inclined mokorotlo hat. He also wore a very long traditional Sotho blanket over his shoulders without a shirt underneath, exhibiting a side view of his solid bulky stature and his metal-like abs and obliques. He had donned black long trousers and white sandals. The blanket nearly covered his feet.

His eyes had three glittering irises, respectively from the pupils, orange, green, yellow. The confusion in his eyes compelled Yoddha to try to calm him down by telling him that Athanasy was nearby. That seemed to have worked, the man smiled hopefully. He thanked Yoddha. He saw the big crowd around them, he looked around as though happy to see more people gathering, then he looked up at Yoddha with a blank expression, he was suddenly like a different person.

Yoddha became alert when he saw the man smirk, but before he could act, an abrupt explosion sourced from the man, it swallowed a wide range of area, blowing up everything near that block — taking out half a quarter of the city. Stomper growled at the mushroom cloud of the explosion. He instantly took off to the scene, he shook the ground when he launched.

CHAPTER 8
BELLUM

There was fire crackling, sirens and alarms going off from afar, civilians out of range of the explosion were in distress. The suicide bomber had killed all the people in that block and severely injured those in the farther vicinity, no corpses or bones could be traced from that block, that part of the city's infrastructure suffered irreparable damage. Athanasy arrived at the scene and quickly used her magic to stifle the fire and blow all the smoke to the sky — the same sky that was raining pieces of Yoddha that had loomed to trap the man.

She found Yoddha enveloped by his shivering dark mass, but he and the mass had so many holes that they looked like Swiss cheese. There were tendrils of the mass on the ground squirming wearily, apparently he had tried to shroud the man so the civilians do not get caught in his explosion, it was quick thinking, but it was not quick enough. Yoddha was breathing heavily and coughing alarmingly, he was hunched over on the ground. Stomper landing on the ground almost caused the damaged tarmac to collapse, the explosion had left multiple fissures on the ground.

Stomper was worried about Yoddha, but Athanasy assured him, "He's badly wounded, but he will survive, his body is already repairing itself," Stomper looked around with ire at the suicide bomber's destruction. He demanded answers from Athanasy, Athanasy attempted to digress, but Yoddha backed up Stomper, and said with short breaths and a hoarse voice, "That man... he was not the same one from the film... he, he did not ex..." he coughed. "He did not die, he escaped..."

Stomper was more shocked than Athanasy was. Athanasy looked up at Stomper's glare, he was expecting answers from her, or he would get hostile with her. She told him, to ease his mind, subtly afraid because she knew he could kill her if he wanted to, "I have a mental image of him from Yoddha's mind, I will use my magic to find him, but right now we need to assure our city of their safety and get Yoddha's wounds tended to. I managed to cut off all outside contact on time. But this city will need answers, and the other cities will know," Stomper's glare remained, but he cared about Yoddha's well-being so he gave Athanasy permission to go do what she had to do, but warned her, "If any more of the Sentinels get hurt or any more of our cities are attacked before you find these two murderers, I will slaughter you along with them." Athanasy was fearful.

The Jackal was already on his way back to the city, while Bullpit and Amanirenas had shortly left on separate clandestine meetings with numerous mayors to address a rising concern of the gradually declining abundance of resources, specifically food.

The doors trundled as Molahlehi opened them, he had a strong smell of fire, which he usually did. He was fresh off his suicide bomber stunt from one of the Sentinels of Anathema's cities. He was bold, to walk into their territory while the Sentinels were present. How confident he was, too, to intentionally grab their attention and expose himself when he could have blown up that city block without them knowing. He was taunting them. That, and also he was very powerful.

He was shirtless, he walked into a very spacious gloom room with a blue glimmer of light that spread to as far as the eyes could see. There was a tall woman on the ramp facing the room leaning against the handrails with her back to him, but nowhere near how tall Molahlehi was. She raised her head and asked Molahlehi, she sounded exhausted, "How did it go?"

Molahlehi stood beside her, and responded, very pleased with himself, "It was marvelous! But this will be our last meeting. They will come after me, I will lure them to a secluded location."

The woman looked at Molahlehi with visible sadness, she had dark circles around her eyes, she hasn't been sleeping. She sighed away the despondence and chuckled. "That sounds dangerous, so it has begun,"

Molahlehi chuckled softly. "Please, it's not like they can kill me. They are measly compared to me. Only Stomper is worth my unfiltered display of might." He narrowed his eyes and said with a distant glare, "I can't wait to take away his power." Before the woman could say anything, the doors behind them trundled again, it was Pygmy. The woman seemed moderately happier to see him, she greeted him with a grin.

"Hi, Shirley. Hi, Molahlehi." Pygmy greeted them with a grin twice as wide as Shirley's when she saw him and waved with both hands, he was a queer one. Shirley admired that about him, she admired a lot of things about Molahlehi and Pygmy because they were the closest things to human beings she could communicate with. She would not be able to spend weeks or even months alone with their secret below the ramp.

Pygmy was abashed, he was wearing casual clothes, he explained, "Sorry for taking long, I had to scrub off the stench, my clothes are still in the washing machine."

Molahlehi asked Pygmy, "So, how was the fight with The Jackal?"

Pygmy hopped onto the handrails and sat on them, he grunted. "I didn't get to fight him. I discovered something during our date in the wild. It appears someone, most likely Athanasy, has been working behind the Sentinels' back. Those things they sent to attack me earlier, The Jackal did not have a clue of their existence, so I deliberately sent him home with some nagging questions."

Shirley grimaced. "Just when you think it can't get any more abhorrent, they prove you wrong," Pygmy nodded.

Pygmy snapped his fingers at the recollection of something, he told Molahlehi, "I made sure The Jackal knows I'm not working alone, so heads up." Molahlehi laughed. "I am fully aware. I just blew up a part of their city. Made sure Athanasy sees me. I tampered with my fire to solely hurt Yoddha and not kill him. I want to have fun with them first." He snapped his fingers at Pygmy at a recollection of something. "Oh, and in other news, this will be our last meeting together. You and I can never set foot here again until our mission is complete." Shirley protruded her bottom lip, now she would be stuck here all alone with their secret below the ramp.

She asked them both, "Make sure you do fast things. I don't wanna be stuck down here with my Alpha AI, it gets lonely and depressing,"

Pygmy inquired, "What happened to your AI boyfriend?"

She responded, "Had to permanently shut him down, he was not performing to my expectations, and he was progressively becoming obsessed and dangerous."

"The drama that follows the pursuit of such things never ends. You should make a TV series that the world can watch after all this nightmare ends." Pygmy sparked an idea in Shirley's head. She gasped and perked up. Her eye was twitching, she said, "It's a bit too late, but I have my dozens of journals, I can get my Alpha AI to generate them to make up for the times I did not record. I shall start recording when I am stuck here while you two have fun."

Molahlehi pensively observed them, his smile was glum. He loved them both so much. He could not wait to watch that crazy series with them after they end the Anathema nightmare, if only he could. He had an idea.

He stretched and suggested, "Since this will be our last meeting in this nightmare, why don't we watch an Odd City marathon together?" Pygmy squealed and jumped with joy from the handrails. Shirley was equally ecstatic. They had both grown fond of Pygmy's favorite show, now it had become their sacred show, just the three of them. It also salvaged the remnants of Pygmy's sanity.

Shirley was wearing shorts with a crop top. Her lean body was synthetic. She had brown skin. She was slim and had very long legs, she had delicate muscles. She appeared slightly older than Pygmy, she somehow looked more like what Pygmy's older sister would like if he had one, she even had a blot on her face to complement his birthmark, but hers was pastel orange like her braids.

She used to cut her braids, but she had not cut them in a while that they grew from the once-consistently maintained bob to a lob. Her synthetic body came to be in order for her to keep up with everything, she created it back when it was just her and Molahlehi but made adjustments to it when Pygmy arrived.

During the second season on the fifth episode, Pygmy had a flashback of that time when he and Pepa were walking together that sunny day when the wind suddenly blew. But the strain of trauma and the years of relentless preparation to attack the Sentinels of Anathema had distorted some of his memories, like how he remembered Felidae as a lioness and not a lynx, he remembered the episode being Pepa's favorite episode. He had pictured the old hag when Pepa told him about it, but now when he thinks back to it he did not understand why Pepa favored that episode so much. His mind was scrambled. At least watching Odd City did not make him cry anymore.

Towards the end of the episode, Shirley noticed a tear on his left eye, but it never trickled down, she didn't think he was even aware of it. She watched him intently before she gave him a tap on the shoulder and whispered to him, "I got you something,"

They were in the living room, which was in a large room divided into three, the other two were Shirley's further divided lab, then the other rooms were where she kept some of her work. There were four sections. She got up from the couch and sprinted into the other room, Molahlehi and Pygmy looked at each other with confusion and shrugged. But Molahlehi was happy, at least the sentiments were there. He couldn't wait to end this nightmare. Shirley returned with a small, neatly wrapped gift box, she sat next to Pygmy and handed it to him with her cheeks faintly pink.

Pygmy thanked her, took the gift box, unwrapped and... like a faucet, some of the lost memories flooded his mind. He remembered that the blurry pink marble Pepa cherished was not really a pink marble. The gift Shirley got him was a necklace of a pink feather inside a marble. He had a loss of words.

Shirley guessed what he would probably ask, since she was very observant of him and Molahlehi. She told him, "16 years ago, a week after the Sentinels of Anathema struck, the last time I went out of this hole, I met you. I had picked up an anomalous radiation coming from the beach, so I tracked it down. That's when I found you, buried in all the rubble with thousands of leeches and dozens of rotten body parts in the area. The leeches did not touch you," now she was becoming emotional, tears began welling up.

"You were all curled up, passed out. The anomaly I tracked down was the divided power of The Jackal inside you. I brought you back here, it took you a couple more days to wake up. When you did, you were so petrified, traumatized, and you couldn't speak. Remember?" She blinked and the tears trickled down, she wiped them and chuckled. "You were such a sweet innocent kid," Pygmy smiled. She continued, "I gave you a journal and asked you to write down all the things you remembered about who you were. You used up three journals. On the many pages you wrote about your time with Pepa, you drew pictures of the marble, and Felidae and a number of disproportionate pictures of Pepa and your parents." She sniffled. "I didn't want to create another lynx for you as a gift so I recreated the feather marble necklace for you. Since we won't be seeing each other until after a while," Pygmy did not know what lynx she was talking about.

Pygmy hugged her and cried, "Thank you so much, Shirley."

Molahlehi was getting emotional watching the two, he had a surprise for Shirley, too. Though, he was feeling bad for them, he pitied them. He waited for Pygmy to put on the marble necklace. Then he called Shirley and told her, "You'll be seeing us more often, because you're leaving this hole with us tomorrow,"

Shirley could not believe it, her gray eyes sparkled as she asked shyly, "Really?" Molahlehi smiled and nodded. She hopped to him and landed with a hug that made him yelp.

She kissed him all over his face as he laughed and begged her to stop. Pygmy giggled on the couch. She paused, but not because Molahlehi asked her to stop, but merely to ask, "Wait, what about the capsules? Who's going to guard them?"

"Your Alpha AI is also down here, along with worker bots. The Sentinels of Anathema do not have the slightest clue of what's happening here so this place is not at all at risk, and it's high time you put those combat skills in that chip in your brain to good use." He replied, she squealed with excitement and bombarded him with endless kisses and 'thank you's'.

Later that night, Shirley and Molahlehi were asleep on the floor, Pygmy had beat them to being the last one awake. Truthfully, his sleep deprivation was something he barely noticed. Sleep was nice, but to him it felt like an escape from everything, a brief break from the morbid reality they lived in, a reality where heaven was only wishful, and as much as he yearned for such an escape, he could not let himself have it as he might end up finding it too comforting and end up getting distracted.

He teleported to the ruined beach house, how magical it always felt when he saw the full moon reflect off the surface of the ocean, the moonlight was perfect for the ambience of his nostalgia. He heard echoes of laughter, two kids, it was him and Pepa, the echoes sounded loud enough that he could hear them in the air, this happened sometimes. Shirley believed it was one of the unfortunate results of his consistent sleep deprivation. He claimed that sometimes felt his parents and Pepa brush against him for a second, and felt Felidae in his arms.

The calming ocean waves that flashed a distinct reflection of the moon here and there when they disappeared, the breeze that gave him goosebumps, the moonlight, it felt exactly like that night Felidae hopped into his room. He had forgotten about his love for '90's music, but if he heard a song from that time, he might remember.

He reached for his pocket and pulled out the marble necklace, he admired its shimmer in the moonlight. He buried it under the beach house, and swore to Pepa he would die and come to the beach house with her to dig it out together, because, "If I take it with me tomorrow, it might get damaged, it's too special to get damaged. Every special thing gets damaged if you expose it to this world for too long." He giggled. "It will be fun when we dig it out together from the other side. Who knows, I might teleport back here moments before my death and hunch over it," he began sobbing, he whispered, "I wish I'd died along with my parents that day."

CHAPTER 9
THREATS

The TV made a quick static noise as the channel changed to the next. Athanasy was on the news, giving a speech in a press conference to address the suicide bomber, almost in every channel, except the typical like the Nat Geo of the animals that used to be, and the music channel, among others. She had accepted that she could not hide what happened, but she could hide what *truly* happened.

She claimed the man was a troubled citizen who had mental perversions that he eventually succumbed to. She even created a false profile and background of him. In the profile, it said Molahlehi had a degree in explosives management, was single, never been married, had no family members in the city, and lived in isolation due to his crippling social anxiety. Though, she did not disclose his faux name. She expressed her condolences to the families who lost their loved ones in the explosion.

There were a bunch of mics in front of her and the typical seamless flashes of lights and clicks. Not forgetting the brand names in the background. There was a chatter when she opened for questions.

One journalist inquired, "What is the name of this suicide bomber?"

Athanasy answered, "We cannot divulge that information out of respect for his extended family members in the other cities."

"Respect?" One blurted. "He murdered dozens and injured multiple, he does not deserve respect."

Athanasy allayed the tumultuous effect that followed the journalist's statement and asked the journalist, "The man does not deserve respect, you may say, but will you be held responsible for his extended family members' persecution after revealing his identity?" The journalist was quiet, so were the others. Athanasy did not use magic to tamper with their poor minds, she merely asked a logical question. She invited the next question.

Another inquiry; "Is this related to the dead communication of the third city? I thought the issue was minor and would be fixed by now, why hasn't it been fixed yet?" This question excited the crowd of journalists and drew in the viewers.

Athanasy skipped a breath and replied, "No, this has nothing to do with that, the communication towers of the third city went offline due to an accident that led to a big fire. They are currently being replaced by new ones. Please bear with the workers who are working tirelessly to install new ones. I assure you, you will be able to communicate with the people from the third city again soon."

More questions flooded, she let them know she would only answer three more questions. The question that followed was from a woman asking her if she was in a relationship at the moment. Athanasy was flattered and bashfully looked at the woman, who was hard to spot with all the flashes. She shook her head, and said no. This aroused the crowd, now everyone was deviating from the purpose of the press conference.

They were asking her out on dates, asking her if she had plans for the weekend, some asked about her and Stomper, luckily there was too much chatter to answer any of those questions. She kindly asked them to quiet down and get back on track so they could continue with the questions. The second last question was also related to her love life, specifically to her sex life, Athanasy laughed with less shyness, she quickly moved on from the question.

"How long will Yoddha be in the hospital?" The last question came from a journalist from the back. Athanasy answered casually, "Yoddha is a Sentinel, so he should be discharged a day or two from now, if not less." They all cheered loudly.

After the press conference.

The Sentinels were already in the boardroom when Athanasy walked in, it seemed they had had a meeting without her. Stomper was standing behind The Jackal with his hand firm on The Jackal's shoulder as though to assure him he was safe. The looks on the other Sentinels' faces when they saw Athanasy made her feel uneasy and suspicious. She had appeared to have walked in on a discourse about her, and not supposed for her.

She asked Stomper, looking around the room nervously, "You started without me? I thought the meeting was not until eleven minutes from now,"

Stomper replied with a grin, "The Jackal was just filling us in on the information he attained from his hunt. Interesting stuff. Take a seat." His voice was wavering between dangerously calm and dangerously threatening.

She sat with apprehension. Stomper immediately demanded, "Where is the man with white hair?"

Amanirenas was mad at Athanasy, despite their somewhat close relation, Yoddha was hurt and she was harboring a lot from them, it seemed. Athanasy was disturbed, she responded, "I don't know, but I did say I can track him. What is going on here? What did The Jackal find out from his hunt?"

Bullpit butted in, "Apparently someone has been experimenting with humans and had sent them to kill the mass murderer."

Athanasy laughed contemptuously. "Please, you think I am the one responsible for that?"

"I spoke with him, the person who burned down our city." The Jackal began, staring into Athanasy's vaguely irritated eyes. "He suggested he was not responsible for the fire — which we now know at the expense of Yoddha. He knows everything. He also seemed to strongly believe we were the ones who created those desecrated humans."

Athanasy perked up. "He knows *everything*? How? Where is he?" Stomper shushed her, and said monotonously as he stared at her with suspicious eyes, "He seems to be able to teleport away. The Jackal can't seem to track him. Funny, he has the same power The Jackal has, yet he can teleport away. The Jackal can't do that. That means he can appear within the cities with numerous bombs, drop them off, and disappear to go yank one off. What irks me the most, though, is who told him everything..."

Athanasy looked at them one by one, their eyes were saying the same thing, she felt insulted. "You all think I told him our secret?" She stood up and propped herself on the table with both hands, she hissed, "How dare you?"

Stomper cocked his head and told her to sit down, she did not for the first second — which she should have, she reluctantly sat down. Stomper commanded, "Just find the white-haired man and find out how many allies they have before they strike again, you do know what will happen if they strike again, don't you?"

Amanirenas and Bullpit did not condone Stomper threatening Athanasy like that. Yes, they suspected her of somehow divulging information to their new enemies and they blamed her for Yoddha's injuries, but they did not wish to harm her. Amanirenas could sit back and let her discomfort sprout, but not Bullpit.

Bullpit spoke up, "Stomper, refrain from threatening Athanasy. Simply because we hold her responsible for the recent incidents, does not mean she is any less of a Sentinel. Keep in mind, it is because of her that we have these powers."

Stomper swiveled his chair to face Bullpit, the look in his eyes was suffused with malice, he laughed at him. He drew closer to the table and threatened Bullpit, "Next time you try to tell me what to do, the Sentinels will be one member short. You hear me?" Amanirenas knew Bullpit would not let Stomper punk him, and the tension had intensified so close to escalating into a tussle. She attempted to mediate; "Athanasy will find those two, The Jackal will have his chance with one, and Bullpit will go after the other. In the meantime, I will personally ensure the cities remain safe, and if there's an attack, I will swiftly handle it."

Stomper leaned back on his chair and adjusted himself, he laughed. "Your girlfriend is smart. And if she fails to protect our people when those two attack... well, let's just hope she doesn't survive the attack." Stomper despised Amanirenas because of her intimidating strength, it irked him, it always have from the moment she exhibited her amazing strength.

When the meeting ended, everyone walked out, Athanasy thanked Amanirenas for sticking up for her, but Amanirenas passed her without a glance at her. Athanasy was disgruntled, and hurried to her suite.

None of the Sentinels liked being near Stomper, he was always hostile and often times abusive and made nasty comments. A couple of years ago, when his displeasure of Amanirenas's might could not be contained any longer, he goaded her to hit him with an energy blast on the face. Amanirenas had refused, this had angered Stomper, he began bumping her and pushing her around. Fortunately, the others had seen this and meddled in to stop him from doing whatever he wanted to do, before Amanirenas defended herself.

Bullpit had a burning desire to fight Stomper, he had invulnerability, Stomper bled. So, he should win the fight, except the only being that was close to rivaling Stomper's monstrous strength was Amanirenas. If Bullpit and Amanirenas ambushed Stomper, they might stand a chance if it would only be a fight without the use of powers. Stomper had a collection of abilities that made him invincible. And he was fast, too. He was a monster, a true demon.

Athanasy did not like Stomper, despite her always engaging in violent sex with him. She had her flaws, she had a thing for powerful men. Them being toxic meant an even better experience in the bedroom. She was using him for sexual gratification, but she hated him so much she wished she never brought him to the Anathema summoning 16 years ago. He had become an unstable, unpredictable threat. But she was working on something.

She went to her disorganized altar and screamed out in frustration at the Sentinels. How dare they question her when none of this would be possible without her? At least Bullpit and Amanirenas stood up for her. She sometimes thought about ambushing Stomper — the only thing that kept her from killing him was that she could not, he was immune to her magic. They had planned to, once.

She had been secretly experimenting on him whenever she would use her spells on him for their aggressive sessions, but even the spells she uses on him have very little effect and almost all the time they never last their intended time. She had a plan to lure in Pygmy and Molahlehi, she could track them using their faces. But she had an idea, perhaps the appearance of these foes might work in her favor.

She collected herself, she thought of how close of a call it was that her human experiments nearly got her project exposed. Truth was she was responsible for those things that went out to assassinate Pygmy, she could track him by his facial features the same way she said she could track Molahlehi from the moment she saw the tape. She had intentionally tampered with The Jackal's mind to have him run in circles without being aware of it while her grotesque "babies" went to gauge Pygmy's abilities, she had what she wanted from their encounter in that skewed building. Now, she would lure him in.

Molahlehi was more of interest to her than Pygmy. He had fire that could severely hurt a Sentinel and vaporize humans. He was a powerful man. He was her type. She just needed to kill Pygmy and bring his head to the Sentinels to regain their trust, then she would search for Molahlehi. She was curious, though, if Bullpit went after him, who would win? Bullpit's skin could not be pierced by anything on this planet, not even a devastating punch from Stomper could contuse Bullpit's skin. Let that unfold as it is meant to unfold, it was time to reach into Pygmy's mind and call for him. She had used his admiration of city lights to lure him to that skewed building – she had not believed it would work, but it did. But it would not work on Molahlehi.

Shirley finished gearing up (she wore the same apparel as Pygmy – but without the breastplate, she had made him those durable clothes and breastplate, and the vambraces – but the barbed wire came with the weapons), she asked Molahlehi and Pygmy to uncover their eyes. She did not know how to pose for them to behold, so she just stood there with a smile and eyes that craved their praises. They were impressed, this pleased her. Although, they were used to her remarkable inventions, they showed utter excitement because she was utterly excited that she was about to go outside for the first time in 16 years.

On her right shoulder there was a gizmo with a barrel, she explained that it shot a piercing laser. Before her left eye hovered a lens that she said contained all sorts of visions. On her left hand she had a big metallic glove with a very small monitor on her forearm. Her right forearm was surrounded by a hovering cylinder that appeared to be holographic, Pygmy asked her how she would shoot it and how she controlled it.

She answered joyfully, "I have enough supply of bullets in a storage case which teleports the bullets into the chambers. It's very small, though."

"What about the glove, and the monitor?" Molahlehi asked. She loved bragging about her inventions, she told them the metallic glove was made of tungsten, but she manipulated its atoms to make it feel less heavy, she also mentioned something about gravity, Molahlehi and Pygmy were lost. She further elaborated that it could launch off her hand and she could control it with the monitor, and that the monitor was also to control her drones which would carry some of the weaponry she would need to exterminate the humans from the many cities the Sentinels owned and protected, and also for her bra.

Pygmy was worried about her safety, she did not have godly power like him, Molahlehi, and the Sentinels, she would suffer critical damage if she engaged a Sentinel. She pulled down her shirt to show them the bra she was talking about, it was a black tactical bra, obviously not a bra but it fit like a bra. She liked the look on Pygmy's face. She explained, "This beauty has multiple features I can control with this monitor, it can form me a force field, turn me invisible, and it has an anti-gravity feature."

On their way up the very long ladder, Shirley told Pygmy she had a surprise for him that pertained his question about her safety in the outside, but hinted that he would have to wait until their mission was complete to see it. Pygmy was excited to see it, but did not think much of it.

CHAPTER 10
HYPOCRISY

Amanirenas sprinted to the elevator Bullpit had just gotten into, he held it open for her. There were a couple of humans around in the floor the Sentinels held their meetings in. When she got into the elevator she stood beside him and thanked him. As the elevator slowly descended the floors, Bullpit noticed Amanirenas was itching to say something. He presumed it was about Stomper, which in a way, it was.

He asked her wearily, "What is it?"

She hesitated, then cleared her throat and whispered, "Remember that time when we had that meeting about you-know-who?" Bullpit gave her the side-eye, he knew what she was talking about, and he did not want to engage in that topic.

"I was thinking," Amanirenas continued, "What if we somehow get these murderers on our side and go on with that plan?"

"What? Are you crazy?" Bullpit asked with irritation. She went on, "The other one we know how he got his powers, but the other one we don't know. We can only assume they know how to summon Anathema. Bullpit, he used fire that can hurt Sentinels, and you know Anathema told us we are immune to fire. I think if we can get them on our side, they might help us kill—"

"Amanirenas, stop!" Bullpit warned her, "We just discussed that they could be working with Athanasy, you heard what The Jackal said about what the other one said about those things that used to be human."

"Right, but there aren't any humans out there, so the humans must have come from here, right? But if Athanasy really is working with them, then why would she send those things to try to kill him?"

"I don't know, maybe they are trying to mess with us."
"No, I don't believe that. If Athanasy—"

"Is working with them to try to kill Stomper, then good for her, I want no part of it. You remember what she said, don't you? She got Stomper to reveal his abilities to her, he has numerous innate abilities and seven techniques, three of which we know of and we know we can't beat him whilst he uses them. Let me remind you of something else; she said he took her outside to show her the fourth one, when she saw it she immediately abandoned the plan to ambush and kill him. She said he said the remaining techniques were too dangerous to use near the cities. And, Amanirenas, he is the only Sentinel immune to Athanasy's mind powers."

Amanirenas retorted, "If they really are trying to kill him, don't you think she knows something about him, now? Like, how to kill him? And how long do you think he is going to keep threatening you until he eventually decides to kill you?"

Bullpit knew the day would come, as the tension between him and Stomper has been progressively leading to that end. Bullpit knew he could just suck it up and tolerate Stomper's abuse like the others, but he was too righteous to do that. Someone had to stand up to Stomper, and that someone would end up dead if they continued. He told Amanirenas, "Look, if you want to get involved in whatever's going on, that's your decision, I won't try to stop you — but leave me out of it. If I do, however, run into either one of those two mass murderers, I'm going to kill them."

Amanirenas was so annoyed. "Are you that stubborn, Bullpit?"

He raised his voice; "Damn it, Amanirenas! They massacred an entire city, and blew up an entire block. We are Sentinels, in case you forgot. We protect and guard our people — we *save* them. These two must pay for what they did. It's our job to make them pay."

Amanirenas laughed derisively. "It's our job, now? We actually protect these people, now? You seem to have forgotten what we did to get to where we are now. The price we paid. That's not what people who protect and *save* people do. And now, there are people who know what we did. You sure you want to kill them for sake of justice or you just want to silence them?"

He leaned in closer to her face. "And what would you rather we do? Tell our people what we did? Let these two and whoever they are working with continue to murder thousands?"

She shook her head in disappointment. "You think you're so righteous. You know what we did is worse than murdering thousands." The elevator beeped open.

Pygmy, Shirley and Molahlehi walked out of the tall grass into the side of the road, with nothing beyond either side but a gas station not far from them and sounds of things skulking in the grass. Molahlehi wished them good luck, and took the side of the gas station while they took the opposite, he stopped walking and told them without looking back, "Everything I do is for a higher purpose. Everything will work out fine. Please don't die."

Shirley thought it was a strange thing to say, but she had lived with him 9 years longer than Pygmy had when he recruited her. She was a brilliant student at Wits

University, furthering her studies in Bachelor of Science for Electrical and Information Engineering and Bachelor of Science in Computer Science.

He had intruded her room one night when she returned late from campus, things nearly ended badly, but Molahlehi displayed his fire manipulation and conjuring abilities to her and told her he needed someone with her unique skills for a higher purpose — that was the first and last time Shirley heard him utter those words, till now. He let her finish all her studies as they built the hideout together in a land he had owned. It wasn't hard for Shirley to believe his presage about Anathema as he had abilities not of ordinary men.

She had a lot of questions about him and his history, but he never indulged in answering any of them. So, eventually she stopped caring about them and focused solely on preparing for the apocalypse. She had managed to create and insert a chip in her brain that connected her to the internet, this nearly killed her, she was rendered disable for months, this had deeply worried Molahlehi.

After she'd healed, right around that time she downloaded all the information she needed to be useful for a post-apocalypse into her brain, which also had its lasting effects, the synthetic her came to be.

She was walking and talking with Pygmy, who seemed oblivious to Molahlehi's words. They had encountered a small herd of large burly guinea pigs and killed them, though not as enthusiastic as when killing humans. And it was purely out of self-defense. Shirley did not wish to remember the first time she killed a person, it was an accident, but there had been numerous 'accidents' that occurred after meeting Molahlehi.

They were walking over a mountain, there was a city on the other side of the mountain. Pygmy volunteered to find the next city while Shirley exterminated that one. She did not mind, before departing, Pygmy asked her what she would use to kill the people within the enormous curtain wall.

"I count twelve thousand people, so I think I'll use an atomic bomb," she said. He looked around, and asked her where the bomb was. She pointed at the sky and told him she had multiple drones way up in the sky carrying heavy artillery. Pygmy looked up, but could not see them, she furthermore explained that they were invisible. That made sense. He hugged her and waved bye. Then, he disappeared.

Athanasy took advantage of this moment – she had sensed his teleportation rousing, she crept into his mind and influenced him to appear in a particular city farther from the one he intended – the spell was weak, but effective. Pygmy would have sensed that something was wrong with his mind, but his mind was scrambled and everything was wrong with it, so he did not sense Athanasy's intrusion. He appeared on top of the curtain wall of another city, ready to wreak havoc, but unlike Shirley, he had to go down there and kill the roughly six to seven thousand people. He did not have the aid of Molahlehi's fire either, this would need him to improve if he were to finish on time and meet up with Shirley.

Suddenly, the humans down there started destroying the communication towers and cutting themselves off from the other cities, some of them got electrocuted and some got burned alive, Pygmy thought that was odd. He walked farther on the curtain wall to get a closer look as sparks and explosions played around in that area. His jaw dropped as he smiled, it seemed they were expecting him.

All of the people, as though one mind, stopped whatever they were doing, froze, and concurrently turned to look up at him. They stood very still. From the ground, Pygmy was practically a dot high on the curtain wall, so ordinarily they should not be able to see him, unless they were looking for him, or one accidentally catches him by looking up.

He disappeared and appeared on top of a low-rise building, which was a foolish thing to do. From everywhere, they all turned as one to look at him. From the building taller than the one he was standing on the roof of, they abandoned their activities, walked up to their windows and watched him. They were dead silent and without an expression, only distant mechanical noises were all one could hear, the ambience was very creepy. He looked around, they were everywhere. He presumed it was Athanasy.

"How'd you know I'd come here?" He inquired, they started gathering around. Athanasy believed exposing herself would not change anything, and would not hamper the plans she had for him.

Athanasy had a ravenous grin as she sat before her altar. She had him, and she would *get* him. The feeling was nigh orgasmic. She promptly contacted the other Sentinels telepathically to alert them, but not all of them, she only called for Bullpit, Stomper, and The Jackal — she had no use for Amanirenas, and given the attitude she was giving her, screw her, she was supposed to have her back and vouch for her.

Bullpit and Amanirenas were at the lobby about to exit the building when she called for him, she mentioned it was urgent, Bullpit asked her what it was, when she mentioned that she had found both mass murderers, Bullpit brimmed with mirth and kissed Amanirenas and rushed back the elevator after relaying to her discreetly that Athanasy had found the two. Unfortunately, she could not tag along, as she had wagered her life on the safety of their people, despite Athanasy having found the two, there were high speculations of them having more allies. And so, she was stuck on guard duty.

Bullpit walked into the boardroom after The Jackal and Stomper, before they sat down they demanded she discloses the locations of the two so they could go after them. She crossed her arms and pressed her lips against each other, Stomper was too ecstatic to burst out in anger, and Bullpit knew no matter what those two do, they would not get away — once Athanasy marks a target, she basically becomes God, as in she has their location indefinitely.

"Well, spill it, will you?" The Jackal impatiently demanded. Athanasy still refused to say anything, and killing her would not have worked as they would be losing their only lead and advantage over Molahlehi and Pygmy. Not that they wanted to kill her. Stomper was the only Sentinel immune to her mind powers, making him the only Sentinel that could beat her on the battlefield, otherwise she could make the other Sentinels her puppets and make them kill each other if she wished, but she respected them, to an extent — she abused her powers the most with The Jackal and Bullpit.

Bullpit knew what he had to do, his questioned righteousness worked in their favor, he sincerely apologized to her for their accusations and told her they were indebted to her for doubting her and would pay her once they kill those two and whoever they were working with. His groveling pleased her.

"I have just shared the location of the one with white hair to you Bullpit, and the kid with dreads with The Jackal. Go kill them and bring their heads. I desire no more to play with him." Athanasy said as she reclined on the chair. Stomper questioned suspiciously, "How certain are you they won't run around?"

"The one with white hair is just standing still, I believe he may be expecting us—or luring us into a trap. So, since Bullpit has invulnerability, he's the perfect candidate if there's a trap. The one with dreads is trapped in the 27th city, I have cast a spell to trap him there. The only exits are the top and the gate, which are both marked with a powerful, impervious seal. And the walls are too thick for his weapons to dig into, he is not going anywhere." She could not mention how she whipped up a spell to counter his teleportation so he does not teleport away, lucky for her Yoddha and Amanirenas weren't in the room, they would have asked her that question.

Stomper persisted he goes with The Jackal, he was convinced Athanasy had in fact messed with The Jackal's mind when he went after Pygmy last time. He knew her inside and out, and I mean very deep inside. She did not contend, but let him know she was also coming with them, as she was not going to sit around while they go out to have all the fun. Stomper still held on to the idea that she may be working with those two, and if he let The Jackal go with her without him there, she and her secret allies would kill The Jackal or do whatever ill plans she had in her sick mind — the very sick mind that always made him hard. But she had a different plan, for him.

CHAPTER 11
MURDER! MURDER!

Pygmy hopped off the building and landed on the street, where the humans there got out of their cars and continued to watch him. They even traced him with their eyes when he jumped off the building, their eyes were locked on him. He was completely surrounded. He looked up at the sky, it looked amiss. He figured Athanasy had used a spell to prevent him from leaving, the joke was on her, he did not want to leave.

He looked around, the humans did not move, they didn't even blink, they just stood there like statues, staring at him. He was too calm, considering he was trapped and surrounded by nearly seven thousand people. He put two and two together, Athanasy knew he had killed those things that had enhanced agility and strength, so she would not try to kill him with ordinary humans — unless she was using their numbers to her advantage. He figured it out, she was stalling him, she was probably on her way with the other Sentinels.

He shrugged. He cast his iklwa and axe high up in the sky and pulled out his short swords. One of them, near him, a skinny older male with a receding hairline and a tired, depressed look on his face started laughing at him. Then he, along with the rest of humans there, suddenly fell to the ground at the same time.

Pygmy looked up to hearing the thump of his weapons hitting a barrier in the sky. All six thousand humans in the city started vigorously convulsing. Pygmy was curious of what was happening. He had an idea. He cast the short swords at the foreheads of two humans near him, the older male and a woman behind him. He caught his iklwa and axe and put them back on his waist. He put his foot on the front of a car and pushed it with his foot, it skidded across the street and ran over five humans, killing them instantly.

He was satisfied, the space was open enough. They started moaning, hissing, and gnarling. He grimaced at them, Athanasy was sick. Their skins began falling off, what concerned Pygmy was what was underneath their skins. They had dark scaly skins. Their nails grew longer and their teeth sharpened. They were changing into... He did not know what they were turning into. He stomped the heads of the dead ones and yanked out his short swords and wielded them. He watched the live ones, they were all breathing heavily, their chests were wheezing. They didn't have noses anymore and their eyes were dully yellow. It was quiet again. Dead quiet, he heard the quiet sounds of his elevated breathing. He clutched his swords tighter.

Glass shattered from the side as sixteen or so of them burst through the windows of the building he had jumped off. He sliced them up one by one with amazing flits. They did not bleed. It seemed they wanted to bite him. As their body parts tumbled on the street, the others rose in unison. He held his short swords in the air, crossed. The look on his face. He was brimming with joy.

They attacked at the same time, he moved fast, he sliced them as he moved around the city. He knew staying in one spot would lead to his downfall. It was hectic, they were coming from every direction that he could not stop for a second. He hopped onto a car and jumped, but another one had hopped off a taller building and was plummeting toward him, he threw his axe right between its eyes, then pulled it out when he passed it as it fell lifelessly to the ground.

He perpetually switched from weapon to weapon — he was using all of his weapons at the same time, he also used his barbed wire, he also had to use his hands and feet. It was incredible how many he was taking down. He wanted to climb the highest building, but he saw many of them standing so close to its windows from within, watching him — waiting for him. One yanked his foot, he lost his balance but managed to kick it off, another one tried to claw his face, but he used his vambrace as a shield. He quickly realized he was not going to survive unless he activated his techniques, and so he did.

There were already seven in motion about to get him, just a single mishap had left him open to seven of those things, this showed how fast-paced things were, especially with these things now having enhanced agility and somewhat bit of enhanced strength. Two hollow dark arms, two barbed skeletal arms and a pair of barbed skeletal feet — they sourced from Pygmy's body. One hollow hand grabbed one of those creatures by the neck and threw it to the other closest one, another hand drew a dagger across the throat of the one before Pygmy's face, the two skeletal arms spun tearing their skins raggedly at contact. Then his skeletal feet kicked one away, whilst the other stomped on the ones that were creeping at low level behind him. He then disappeared from the spot as he had seen too many gathered there.

He appeared farther away on a basketball court. They were everywhere! The ones that were in that vicinity spotted him and attacked. His distorted, ghastly face returned to normal as the skeletal limps sank back into his body. The hollow arms remained, though, wielding a short sword and the iklwa in their hands while his wholly visible hands wielded another short sword and the axe. He had one dagger on his mouth, his teeth firm on the handle. Some of them hopped over the fence while others trampled it. They shook the ground.

Soon there were too many bodies in the basketball court and they were becoming cumbersome. He jumped to escape, another one jumped at him, but it was too slow so he stepped on it to boost himself. There were more in the sky, five of them, aiming at him. He landed on a tree, they landed on the basketball court as corpses. He disappeared as more flooded the tree.

He reappeared somewhere else in city, he swiftly killed the few that were creeping around.

He heard the ground tremble. He turned and saw them stampeding toward him, eerily similar to the zombies from one of the best zombie movies ever made, in my opinion, *World War Z*. They were coming in all directions, some hopped off buildings.

He was really trapped, but he was having the time of his life. He swiped his arm at them, a humongous sword with a vantablack blade swiped them away, wrecking the near buildings along. He turned and swiped again to the other two directions, another humongous sword claimed the second and the third stampede in one swipe. But unfortunately, his victory was short lived, there were still more coming, and they were clogging the street.

He hopped off the ground and killed the ones that had leaped off the building with his back against clogged street. He landed on his shins and slid like soccer players do when they celebrate a goal, still with his back at them, then jerked his torso backward nigh in a wheel pose, the two humongous swords reigned down on the stampede, breaking the tar and causing the road to cave in.

Pygmy admired his work. Though the humongous vantablack swords were very effective, there were a number of survivors. Pygmy darted, using his teleportation to kill them, after every kill he disappeared and appeared to another creature to kill it. This was a very effective strategy. It lit up an idea in his troubled mind. He started skipping and hopping from building to building luring the never-ending populace toward the tallest building in the city, he spotted those that waited for him. On his way there, he killed a number of the creatures that almost got him.

As he was nearing the building he looked down and saw the roads were teeming, well, these things were teeming the entire city. His hollow arms pushed forward as though doing a push up on an invisible wall. The two humongous swords cleared the way, they crossed outward like two opposing windshield wipers. Then they disappeared. Pygmy looked behind him and saw quiet a large number of those things, this made him so happy that he nearly cried. There were some behind the tallest building and some on either side despite all those that were in his way being wiped out by the swords.

When he reached the bottom of the tallest building, he resummoned his gigantic swords and cut off the two pillars that held the building up from the front leaving the two at back, then he disappeared. The building fell and crushed the hundreds that he had lured there, the collapse also killed most of the ones that were in that building. Dust blew everywhere. The building also crashed into other buildings and killed so many of the creatures. The total kill from that trick had to be nearly a thousand, if not more.

Pygmy had an idea. He appeared and disappeared around the city destabilizing the taller buildings to fall and crush the creatures. By the time he was done, nearly the entire city was in ruins, and the air was heavily moted. He lodged his weapons into the side of the curtain wall with his hollow hands and held himself up there as he watched the buildings tip over and the city collapse. He was almost done, there were some survivors, he tugged out his weapons and ran down the wall. His hollow arms disappeared, he did not need them anymore. He could kill the survivors with just his weapons and his two arms.

Stomper, The Jackal, and Athanasy were nearing the city, they could see a cloud of dust coming from the city. Stomper was ahead of them as he was flying high in the sky. Athanasy was flying near the ground beside The Jackal, who kept a considerable distance between himself and her. He did not want her fiddling with his mind. Though, she might try, she would not do so in the presence of Stomper, plus she had no motive. She began soaring and lifted The Jackal off the ground. Stomper stomped and stood at the top of the curtain wall, distraught by the sight Pygmy had left.

There were no survivors. The city was in an irreparable state. There was a big crevice on the other side of the curtal wall. Stomper did not understand. Pygmy had used his massive vantablack sword to cut through the wall and make his escape. When Athanasy and The Jackal reached the top of the curtain wall, they were appalled by the sight. Athanasy's plan for Stomper was to manipulate

Pygmy and The Jackal to attack him. She sensed Pygmy was still close.

Stomper turned and grabbed Athanasy by the throat, The Jackal flinched. Stomper yelled at her, "You said he would not be able to escape. I told you what would happen to you. Where is he? Are you working with him?" Athanasy's face quickly turned pink, she could not speak, he was squeezing her throat. She started flailing, but quickly grew too weak.

The Jackal was not comfortable with this, he did not know what to do, he did not want Athanasy to die, but he could not stand up to Stomper. Athanasy was confounded, she had no clue what Pygmy had used to escape, she did not know about his techniques, which she should have visited when she crept into his mind.

The sky shook as multiple cities were hit with atomic bombs, they could see the mushroom clouds from two cites even from that vast distance. Stomper gasped and let go of Athanasy, she fell to her back and was desperately gasping for air, tears were falling down her face. Stomper believed this was Molahlehi's doing. He looked down at Athanasy, his suspicions were confirmed, or so he thought, he indubitably believed she was working with Molahlehi and Pygmy.

Poor Athanasy was too weak to cast a spell and too distracted, and like that — before she could suggest influencing Pygmy back to that city, Stomper stomped his foot on her head, crushing it and killing her. He believed she sent Bullpit on a wild goose chase while her other accomplice blew up the other cities. But the atomic bombs were Shirley's doing. The Jackal looked at Athanasy's corpse in horror and disbelief, he was shivering with fear. He was too scared to look Stomper in the eye, he wanted to run away. Stomper was a psychopath.

Stomper picked up Athanasy's corpse, his hand fit her entire upper arm, and threw it down the curtain wall into the ruined city. He burst it into countless pieces, she got popped into nothing but blood, in case she tries to regenerate herself.

Stomper then proceeded to instruct The Jackal to go to the farther city and he would go to the farthest city, "The white-haired man must still be around there. We'll find him and kill him, too. Then we'll find his accomplice and whoever else is working with them."

The Jackal stuttered. "St—S—Stomper... y—you kill—k—k—ki—killed h—h—her..."

Stomper did not have the patience for this, Molahlehi was going to escape. He walked closer to The Jackal, his demeanor suggested he was going to kill The Jackal as well. He said in a calm tone, "The deranged boy with the malicious grin killed her and got away. Now, I don't want him to kill you, too, so get to it, now! If the white-haired man escapes, don't come back to any of the cities."

The Jackal's legs were so wobbly that he fell, Stomper forcibly picked him up. He quickly chased after the farther burning city, Stomper launched to the farthest one. But when they arrived and scoured the next six cities, there was no trace of Molahlehi nor Pygmy, and slowly the tracker in The Jackal's mind quailed as Athanasy was no more. The point of scouring the cities was to hopefully find the other accomplices as they had already placed trackers to Pygmy, so there was no rush to chase after him.

The Jackal did not rush to notify Stomper, instead he chased after Pygmy's faint location. The location in Stomper's mind disappeared moments after he took Athanasy's life, this might have been due to his immunity to her powers. Or it was simply just her doing, the only way to know would be to ask Athanasy, but they could not do that.

CHAPTER 12
AZRAEL'S VISIT

As all the horrors were unfolding, Amanirenas was standing on top of the curtain wall of their most valuable city, the city was the sole city that produced and distributed oil, the 16th city. Amanirenas had thought about it, and had concluded that this city should be her priority, as if the two mass murderers and their accomplices target it, it would cause stagnation and the possible collapse of all remaining cities unless the Sentinels find other places to mine for oil — and that was not easy to do.

She stood with her arms crossed and a sullen look on her face. The wind was blowing moderately, making her hair and wings wave to its direction. None of the people down there noticed her, and she preferred it that way, she was in no mood to face them and continue pretending she was a savior of their people. They had secrets, and there were people who knew their secrets, dangerous people. She was meditating on her short conversation with Bullpit from the elevator, and what Bullpit had said when he hurried back to the elevator.

She had been wanting an out for a while, and this might be her only chance. She could flee from the Sentinels and form an alliance with those two, except those two wanted her and the Sentinels and all their people eradicated. She thought about how it was worth a try, living around Stomper was hell, he despised her for her strength, and despised Bullpit for not letting him push him around. Another thing that haunted her was his depraved desires, but they never defied him or tried to put a stop to it, that made them monsters, more evil than what those two are trying to kill them for.

In an unsuspecting city about three cities away from the one Amanirenas was guarding.

The sky had already started darkening, and there were sudden strong winds. The kids were looking up through windows in their classrooms, people were stopping their cars and walking out to see, the construction workers stopped working and looked up with apprehension, some people turned away from their TV screens and walked outside to see what was happening. This was an impending attack.

There was one couple, two adolescents who had bunked school to go to the mall and splurge the boyfriend's money on the girlfriend's insatiable materialistic desires, the boyfriend was squandering his parents' money for the girl not because he loved her, but solely so he could get with her and later on brag about it to his friends. The girlfriend was also using the boyfriend for his wealthy parents' money so she could brag to her friends about getting the latest expensive phone. Little did the guy know he was not going to get anything. They were walking on the side of the road carrying a lot of bags with the logos of the most expensive stores in the city. They stopped on the sidewalk to gaze at the sky.

There was a loud thud, some splatter, tires of a car screeching, people screaming in terror, then the distracted driver ended up crashing into a traffic light after running over more pedestrians. The expensive clothes fell to the crimson ground like leaves off a tree.

On one side of the city, there were a couple of rich folks at the exclusive swimming pool with glass walls at a very exclusive hotel that most of the people who lived in the city could not even afford. Most of the people at the pool were older men with younger women, older women with younger men. They were playing in the pool with a beach ball, giggling altogether like little kids.

The waiters and waitresses were fit and obscenely sexualized. One young man had been fired and reported to have gone missing after he tried to open a case against an older woman who allegedly drugged him and, well, yeah. The old women on the pool loungers who had been basking in the sun sat up nervously and stared at the obscuring clouds. The beach ball ended up falling over and down 65 storeys.

At the bottom. The doorman was standing beside a crowd staring at the sky with apprehension, he caught the beach ball, there was a married couple in a convertible that had just stopped before the hotel. They were married, but not to each other. They looked up at the sky, the man took off his sunglasses. Then, alas! Lightning struck the pool area and all from above, along with the shattered glass, fell. There was a common reaction among those at the bottom. Shards of glass pierced those who could not get away on time, the people that fell 65 storeys splattered on the ground, on the cars, and onto other people turning each other into mash.

The people near the hotel started screaming and running for shelter. The adulterous woman had managed to elude the falling glass and people. She screamed at the top of her lungs at the sight of the gory conjointment of her adulterous partner and a senior citizen who had fallen from the sky, her hands were shivering before her face. Someone bumped her when everyone was running around in panic and she fell on the ground. Before she could get up, a beach lounger fell on top of her, snapped her out of shape and killed her instantly.

The doorman was bleeding profusely on the ground, the panicking crowd had stabbed him and pushed him over when he refused to let them into the hotel lobby. He crawled away from those stampeding into the hotel, but the wound was too deep, he did not make it. The thing that caught the people's attention was not the black clouds, they had seen black clouds before. The thing that caught their attention was the dark figure that was manifesting above their city. It was a humongous shadow figure hunched over their city.

Soon, the tall gates of the city were teeming with violent, terrified people attempting to get away, the security guards were killed without being given the chance to move away for the stampeding crowd. The code to open the gates was not working, it was hacked and rendered useless, the people ended up smashing the keypad and tried to force the gates open, but it was futile, the gates were designed to be strong enough to be broken down by the Sentinels of Anathema, to keep out danger when the sun set.

The manifesting figure started becoming more and more distinct. Back in the 16th city, thanks to the communication towers not being destroyed, the whole thing was being covered on the news, and it appeared on every channel and was shown on all jumbotrons.

Amanirenas flew down to get a better view of what was being streamed live from that city. There was a crowd that quickly grew below that was made up of petrified viewers. Amanirenas was levitating before the biggest jumbotron, she was, like the rest of those who were watching, intrigued and glued to the screen to see what the terrifying figure was becoming. There was a chatter below. If Athanasy were there she would have prevented this, Amanirenas thought, but this was being shown in every single city they protected. It was chaotic.

She opened her cape wings and bolted to that city when she saw what the figure had manifested into. It was a dead, hooded figure with an eerie grin. Its osseous arms were sparsely draped with bits of flesh vainly clinging onto the bones. It was the Angel of Death. He was holding something.

He was holding an enormous pale green gas cylinder with a toxic sign and a warning sign on it. The screams from below were not pleasant, they were traumatizing, those watching from their TVs, smartphones, and jumbotrons would not sleep a wink due to those harrowing screams of terror. Amanirenas was flying as fast as she could, she had passed over the other cities and was nearing this one, she could see the half-body Azrael figure hunched over the city, she immediately shot her energy blasts at him. She was befuddled when she saw them merely go through him.

She cried, "No!" with tears in her eyes. She reached out her arm at the gas cylinder as she watched it fall from the Angel of Death's osseous hands.

She reached the city and instead of attacking Azrael again, she chased down the toxic gas cylinder. She headed underneath it and managed to stop it before it could reach the ground. It wrecked the upper parts of some of the buildings and fractions of those buildings fell and crushed some people. All those watching gasped, then there was silence. The toxic gas cylinder was 300 feet in width and 600 feet in length, and filled with toxic gas, so Amanirenas was barely holding on.

She was wondering why the gates weren't opened yet. The toxic gas cylinder was too heavy for her, her hands started causing dents on its surface as it weighed down on her. She could use one hand to blow the tall gates open with her energy blasts, but that would not give the people below enough time to escape before the toxic gas cylinder overpowers her one hand and falls.

She did not want to think of what would happen if it made contact with the ground, she could gently put it down, but that might detonate it, she could not risk it. She screamed laboriously as her hands caused deeper impressions, this meant she could not fly it upward, she would pierce through it. There was no way out.

She looked down at those terrified faces down there, they were all looking up to her. They did not want to die, their cries would haunt her, and those looks on their faces, as well. Those from afar were celebrating her being able to stop the toxic gas cylinder, but the ones that were near that could see her, knew their demise was pending. So did the ones who were watching from other cities know this.

Amanirenas's face was pink, it looked like it was about to explode. Her veins were bulging, she was starting to sweat. The dents swallowed her forearms, forcing her to bend forward. She looked down at those faces. Those poor faces. She started crying, she could not let them die. There was a little boy near an ice cream truck, his ice cream had fallen over. He was separated from his mother during the havoc. He held on to his cone, his face was flooded with tears and his mouth flooded with mucus.

Amanirenas wanted to shut her eyes and look away from his, there was nothing she could do for him. Maybe if she lets go of the gas cylinder she could swoop down and whisk him away before the toxic gas is released, but what about the other kids? The viewers were also crying and praying for that city.

Then, Amanirenas's ears turned deaf, she could not hear anything as the weight of the toxic gas cylinder disappeared, not just its weight, but the toxic gas cylinder itself disappeared, but the shadow over the city was not gone, so she knew it had not disappeared. She saw from everyone's faces looking up in horror. She looked up, the Angel of Death had lifted it not too high, then he let it go. It fell down on Amanirenas, she managed to stop it at a different surface without dents, but the surface making contact with her strong hands caused new dents. She was brought closer to the ground by the weight, and she was losing stamina.

Those farther away who were oblivious before thinking she had rescued them had a rude awakening. Panic pervaded. Amanirenas was bedrenched in sweat, and she began hyperventilating. She refused to let the toxic gas cylinder reach the ground, she did not care if it was inexorable, she would fight to save her people for as long as it took. One of the other Sentinels might arrive, but which one? Yoddha was in the hospital, Athanasy was dead, Stomper and The Jackal went after Pygmy, Bullpit went after Molahlehi. No one was coming.

Her ears deafened one more time as the Angel of Death lifted the toxic gas cylinder again, the weight being lifted off her caused her to collapse to the ground. The viewers gasped, some were sobbing. Some of the people around her started pushing her and pulling her and begging her to get up and save them, but she could not hear them, she was exhausted, her body was giving up on her.

She exhaustedly raised her arms to target the gates and amassed enough energy to blast the gates wide open, but unfortunately, the worst thing happened. The Angel of Death had raised the toxic gas cylinder higher into the sky, and instead of dropping it, he shoved it down at the city.

By the time the energy blasts blasted those gates out, the toxic gas cylinder hit the ground and the toxic gas spread like an explosion, killing everyone not just at first inhale, but also instantaneously eating away their skins at first contact. The toxic gas blew out through the destroyed gates and spread out farther outside, it even rose up and covered the entire city and reached high for the sky.

The viewers cried as most of the communication to the city was lost. They were wondering where the other

Sentinels were and why they did not help Amanirenas. They were even more angered, how could they let this happen to the people they were entrusted to protect? And they were distraught by the death of Amanirenas. From the cameras and smartphones that were still functioning, nothing could be seen, just the dark misty green gas, it was impossible to see anything.

Amanirenas had shot out of the city at moment of impact, she had inhaled a bit of the toxic gas. She was powerless, coughing out blood on top of the curtain wall, the Angel of Death had magically disappeared. Her eyes were burning. She had no more energy in her. She was not human so the toxic gas would not kill her, unless she is exposed to it for a longer period of time.

It was not over, her eyelids were shutting by themselves, as the toxic gas that reached up to the sky was lumbering towards her, she crawled like the doorman, she crawled to the edge of the wall and peeked over, the toxic gas she had let out when she blew those gates was spreading everywhere.

She had planned on jumping off the wall and letting herself pass out – she would survive the fall, but now if she did that she would get killed by the toxic gas. It was even detrimental to the plants, the few mutated animals scurried from it.

She tried to get up, but she fell to her knees and forearms, she looked behind her and saw the toxic gas getting closer to her. She was panting, blood was still coming out of her mouth. She used her final might to angularly blast off the edge of the curtain wall and shot to the sky, her launch caused an impression on the edge of the wall.

She lost conscious in the sky, but had turned behind to see, she was far from the city and the toxic gas. Her eyelids shut and she plummeted to the ground.

CHAPTER 13
HIS DEPRAVED DESIRES

Yoddha woke up from his bed, the inside of his body had erratically shifting spots of mass that made him feel light and heavy, but he was fully healed. He was facing the TV at the corner of the room, there was a nurse who watched the screen in disbelief, when Yoddha focused his attention on the screen, which initially made his eyes hurt, he saw the headline read *'AMANIRENAS DIES TRYING TO SAVE CITY!'*

This made Yoddha snap into being wholly awake, he exclaimed something that startled the now weeping nurse and she dropped her clipboard. His hair ran across his face, he asked the nurse with urgency, "When did that happen? What else happened while I was out? How long was I out?"

The nurse continued weeping, she then collapsed to her shins. Yoddha could not believe that Amanirenas was dead, he had to go to the tower to find out what else had occurred. On the news it also showed helicopters flying around the city that had fallen victim to the toxic gas, the helicopters were scouring for Amanirenas's body. They declared her dead when a small group wearing gas masks that tried to land into the city to search for her and any survivors got vaporized by the toxic gas at first touch. Yoddha asked the nurse where his clothes were, she was still weeping, he shook his head at her and went on to ask someone else.

Stomper's clenched fist trembled in rage as he stared down at a flooded city as the scorched bodies of the civilians bopped on the surface. There were electric discharges that continued to burn the corpses further. There were no survivors. Someone had drowned them all, and it seemed the flood wasn't the only thing that took them out, adding electricity to the mix did the trick. It was Shirley, the Angel of Death was also Shirley. Locking the gates and filling the inside of the city with water would have took long for Pygmy and Molahlehi, if they could have achieved it at all.

Stomper was furious, he was certain that Athanasy had more accomplices, not just two, as this was the seventh city that's been destroyed (to his count).

It did not matter how fast he flew, he never arrived on time, it seemed all from this group of mass murderers could teleport. Shirley was using her highly advanced tech for these atrocious acts, what Stomper did not know was that the tech was still hovering above the city, above him, invisible high in the sky. He let out a viscous scream and blasted off to return to the main city.

Another thing that occupied his mind was The Jackal, he believed if he could not get these elusive monsters, then

The Jackal had no chance. He had warned him not to return to any of the cities if he did not find the boy with the malicious grin, he knew The Jackal revered and feared him, but after murdering Athanasy in front of him, he might squeal, especially since he now had nowhere to go.

Stomper could fly, so he would arrive in the city first and convince everyone The Jackal is working with those two and that they killed Athanasy before he gets the chance to expose him for Athanasy's murder — but that would be his word against his, and since their people believed Athanasy and Stomper were a couple, they might believe Stomper over The Jackal. Even if they do end up believing The Jackal, Stomper would harass and murder him and threaten the other Sentinels to say The Jackal confessed to killing Athanasy and later on committed suicide as he could not live with the guilt anymore.

The flower shop was teeming with people, there were so many people getting flowers for Amanirenas at the city Amanirenas was last before she blasted away to her doom. The owner of the flower shop was giving out flowers for free. People were gathering at the center of the city right in front of the city's biggest jumbotron and were leaving flowers in a big, adorned circle. Some put the things they valued most. The mood was gloomy, people were mourning Amanirenas in every city except the ones Shirley disposed of, in the others, though, she had cut out communication.

It was unclear why she did not destroy the communication towers at the city where she exhibited the Angel of Death, she may have intentionally lured one of the Sentinels there as she knew the toxic gas could also harm Sentinels (as its chemical compound was made with the surreptitious help of Molahlehi), so even if more than one had come, they would have gotten themselves killed. She had not bet on Amanirenas arriving, but a win is a win.

One man had managed to get his hands on the biggest bouquet, he lifted it up so it does not get smushed by the depressed crowd bumping into each other here and there. When he finally reached the beautiful circle of flowers, he crouched and gently placed the bouquet next to the others, unintentionally upstaging the smaller flowers.

He got up and stared despondently at the displayed picture of Amanirenas on the jumbotron. Another man beside him wearing a beret commented, "She was the best, wasn't she? A real superwoman. I once hugged her, one cold night a few years back. It was snowing. I found her on the roof of that building there," he pointed at it, the man did not turn to look at it, "She was crying." His eyes turned red and moist, the other man was now listening.

The man with the beret continued, "I was going out for a smoke, I was shocked when I saw a Sentinel crying. I asked her what was wrong, she turned when she saw me and she tried to blast off, but I think she wanted someone to see her. I don't know. When I asked her what was wrong for the second time, she said she just needed a hug, so I hugged her. Then right after she thanked me she left."

The man who was listening thought he was lying, why would a Sentinel cry? He nodded at him and turned to walk away, but then their arms had become conjoined, their eyes widened as fear grew inside them. Another person, walking by, accidentally stepped on the man's shoe, then, their feet also conjoined. There was a sudden scream of a woman from the other side of the crowd, then some murmurs, then fear disseminated as the crowd began conjoining. Some tried to run away, but were pulled into the conjointment by a force like metal to a magnet.

Their clothes started tearing off as the conjointment grew and more victims were pulled into it. Some were helplessly flailing while some desperately reached their arms out for help. There were screams of terror, as those kinds of screams were becoming a norm in this terrifying world. The people grew to a buck naked 16-foot blob monster that resembled the one Pygmy was inside of, some had thankfully managed to escape before they got sucked in. Some of those who escaped did not turn back – they just continued running without glancing back while others who escaped stopped and took out their phones to livestream this.

There had been news reporters recording the mourning of Amanirenas live and interviewing some of the people regarding Amanirenas, some of their camera people had managed to get away just in time, they recorded this giant blob. Those who continued running took the beeline to the tall gates, they did not want to end up like those in the city where Amanirenas died.

Before things could escalate, the bellowing of the blob turned into a reverberating voice of a woman, a voice they recognized, a voice that made them stop trying to escape. It was Athanasy's voice. She spoke to them, "My people, it is I, Athanasy. I deeply apologize for the way I chose to communicate," she saw the flowers on the ground, she had inadvertently crushed some, she did not know what was happening.

Yoddha had just found his clothes and was putting on his shoes on the waiting chairs when he saw this on the news, everyone in the hospital stopped and watched, some were nauseated by the sight and vomited. It was hard to see where the mouth was with all those folds of fat. Yoddha was so confused. He whispered under his breath, "Just what the hell is going on?"

Athanasy continued, she appeared on every jumbotron, smartphone, and every TV screen, except the jumbotron behind her, the one that still had a picture of Amanirenas. "I bear very terrible news, I stand before you in this form as I have been killed and will not be here any longer,"

Everyone gasped, others covered their mouths in shock, some put their hands on their head, there were mixed reactions.

One older woman cried out to her, "How many Sentinels are we going to lose in a day?" this caused a disgruntled chatter. Athanasy turned with difficulty to look at the jumbotron behind as one child pointed behind her.

She was devastated when she saw a picture of Amanirenas, so the flowers were for her. Athanasy briefly forgot what she wanted to say to the people, she could not believe it. How could Amanirenas die? She moaned, she was in pain, not just the physical pain of the anguished people she had merged, but also the physical pain that felt like a nail piercing the heart. She and Amanirenas were not on good terms the last time she saw her, and they were really close, she had planned on fixing things when she'd return with Stomper and The J— Of course, that!

She turned with the same slow difficulty to face the people and paused to stomach the pain. She urgently told them, "I apologize for not being here, I should have been here, I wish I could have been here, but I couldn't because Stomper took me out to a city he'd destroyed and killed me." A common, nigh unison unpleasant reaction. She went on. "Yes, this is true. The truth is..." she sighed, one person encouraged her to come out and say it. "The truth is we have been under attack by a group of people with the same power as us who have been working with Stomper, the man with the white hair who nearly killed Yoddha was not a lonely man from another city, he was Stomper's accomplice.

"This group destroyed the city we lost communication to, so I worked hard to find them, I left with The Jackal and Stomper when I located them to bring them to justice, but when we arrived there, Stomper revealed that he was working with these people and asked me to join them, when I refused and threatened to expose him, he killed me. I don't know if The Jackal is also working with them, or if he's even still alive."

Everyone was stunned, Yoddha was angered by this, but he was even more confused. Athanasy asked the people from the main city in the tower to share a mysterious tape and "evidence of Stomper's true nature" and gave the people a heads up that the scenes were very graphic and disturbing, and apologized in advance, but she had to do this, the people deserved to know the truth.

She continued as her assistant from the main city's tower worked on sharing the tape and the evidence with everyone, "The Sentinels of Anathema have lived in constant fear of Stomper, he is constantly threatening us, he dictates and if we try to defy him he becomes violent. I know you all believed he and I have been in a perfect relationship, but I have been suffering under the unbearable abuse of this tyrant for many years.

"The Sentinels and I have tried to find ways to stop his constant abuse of his power, but he is immune to my powers and he overpowers all of us. My people, Stomper is not your hero, he is a monster."

Stomper flew into the main city to rush to the tower when he heard Athanasy's voice everywhere in the city, he stopped in the sky, watching in fear of her exposing him for murdering her. At the same time, pictures of his depraved desires were exhibited on the screens. In every picture, he is shown feasting upon the viscera of a different human from the different cities in the same dark room — he was a messy eater. The pictures were gory and disturbing. The people began recognizing those in the pictures, they were the many different people who had been reported missing and never found on the occasions the people partied outside the walls and took tours around the forsaken world — which suspiciously did not stoke Anathema or Mother Nature, most of them had gone missing on their way from one city to another but were claimed to have been eaten by the animals outside the walls. The people everywhere in the remaining cities had a common reaction.

One person spotted Stomper in the sky and alerted the others, they turned to look up at him and started swearing at him, calling him names, and telling him to leave. As this was happening, some of the screens showed Stomper in the sky in that city, now everybody could see him. Then the screens were shared between him, Athanasy, and the tape of Pygmy murdering an entire city of people that he set ablaze.

Athanasy spoke, "This is one of his accomplices. Stomper's thirst for human blood is insatiable. I can only assume now he wants to eat entire populations from each city. Before he became a Sentinel of Anathema, Stomper was an infamous cannibal – I thought I could change him..."

She even shared the tapes from his previous life as a human, the graphic pictures did not stop coming. The people below him started throwing things at him, he roared at them, then, he used his powers to blow up the tower — causing the screens to go blank, then blasted to where Athanasy was. Athanasy succinctly told the people of the city she was in, "You see, he's a monster! These people I have merged will go back to normal once I disappear." She stared into the cameras and beseeched, "Please, if there are any Sentinels still alive, please save our people from this monster. I beg of you!"

Everyone in that hospital turned and looked at Yoddha, they were depending on him to save them. He was the only Sentinel guarding the cities. The people were scared, everything was falling into chaos. Yoddha knew he could never hope to beat Stomper in a fight, he had to find Bullpit to raise the odds.

He sighed, there was nothing else he could do, he might as well go die a heroic death since the Sentinels were dying anyway. Plus, from now on Stomper would create a world under his ruthless hand, he would probably force the people to submit to him and worship him and if they refuse he would slaughter them, Yoddha did not want to live in such a world. He ran out of the hospital, his black mass stretched to the sky and began morphing into a gigantic gaunt creature. It looked like a centipede, but with elongated legs, the people cheered as he hurried to the curtain wall with his hundred legs. He was actually riding this odd-looking creature.

Athanasy was still talking to her people when she suddenly bloated and burst. Blood and a very thick fluid with a foul smell squirted everywhere, the merged organs, bits of limbs and heads of those who had gotten merged were shot out in all directions. It was Stomper, he had used his space-benders to blow them up. He stopped in the sky above them. Another thing Athanasy had used to her advantage, she knew those people would never go back to their normal human form, she had bet on Stomper killing them, which saved her from being labeled a murderer.

"You demon! You're not a hero!"

"Go back to where you came from!"

"We don't want you here! Leave!"

"You will die a very painful death!"

"Get out! You're not welcome here! Leave!"

"You murdered those people in that tower!"

The people raged on.

There were two cops who shot at him, he turned to look at them, their bullets just bounced off his skin.

He screamed at all of them, "I am your god! You will kneel before me and continue to serve me, whether you like it or not!" Some of them ridiculed him and laughed at him. Some started booing him, some started throwing bigger stuff at him. He was furious, he started murdering them one by one. Everyone witnessed from all the cities.

CHAPTER 14
THE FACES THEY MAKE

The remaining 23 cities witnessed Stomper slaughtering an entire city, if there were any doubt that he and the kid (who was actually 24 years old) with the malicious grin and the man with white hair were accomplices, it would quail. He could have used his terrifying abilities to cut communication with the other cities and isolate this one, but he wanted to send a strong message to those watching.

Despite not standing the faintest of chances against Stomper, the measly people fought to the death — which was very imminent. They were fighting for Athanasy and for Amanirenas. They were fighting for their freedom from the demon they had revered as their god and sentinel. That would be a pretty historic moment, wouldn't it? They *were* fighting for freedom, but not in the way one might think.

Some mayors of the remaining 21 cities had decided the people had seen enough to be disillusioned from Stomper being their savior and turned off the livestream throughout their respective cities. There was honestly no need to further taunt the people with such harrowing scenes. Stomper let out a raucous roar that thundered throughout the city, splattering thousands and blowing away the city's infrastructure into fragments in mere seconds.

He stood in the ruined city, it was red with blood. He had inadvertently cut out the live stream. He looked around, there were some couple of thousands of survivors, he did not need to continue wasting time, he wanted the 20 remaining cities to witness his massacre. He blasted to the sky and used one of his vague abilities to cause the entire city to cave into the ground. There was a sudden abyss under the city, he watched indifferently as his once-faithful followers fell into the maw of darkness. All that food, gone.

He looked around, he had to find a city that could broadcast his message, he knew what he would say to those watching, he had dreamt of his day for months. He had grown weary of pretending, he could still use lethal force and still get the people to hold him in high regard. He would make them all bow down to him, one by one, then, he would get them to procreate and once old enough to handle heavy duty, he would force their offspring to work under horrendous conditions like their parents and grandparents. He would pay them by giving them one off-day every quarter of the year.

He did not care how many he had to kill to build his dynasty as the sole Sentinel of Anathema, he was almost sad that he had to kill Yoddha, as far as he knew, he and Amanirenas were the only Sentinels in the now 19 cities (one less thanks to him). He could not wait to get his hands on Amanirenas.

Shirley continued decreasing the cities to 15 cities, she had heavy weaponry of mass destruction swarming the skies and no one noticed. She had stopped to sit down and watch the whole Athanasy and Stomper's lovers quarrel from a different city, it was very entertaining. She remotely reduced the number of cities, and people were so absorbed into Stomper killing en masse, so the very few cities that caught up to what was happening in the other cities' reports barely went noticed.

The Stomper situation upstaged Amanirenas's death, the Angel of Death, and the rapidly dropping cities.

Something was bothering Shirley, and it was not killing hundreds of thousands of people. Pygmy had said they were not innocent, but that did not seem likely, but they had their firm convictions. She tracked Pygmy while dropping this cities' numbers one by one. Of course she had put a tracker on him, and without consent, but she had failed to put one on Molahlehi, which would not have been for the same reasons she deemed necessary to put one on Pygmy.

She did not know if she trusted Molahlehi the way Pygmy did, maybe because he was too obscure, or because he was the reason she had killed numerous people and slipped away from her humanity, way before Anathema struck.

As she was making her way to the city Pygmy was in, Stomper had reached another city, killed half the population, and declared himself their new god and threatened to kill more who would refuse to bow down to him. If they all refused he would be forced to annihilate the remainder of the human race, then no one would be left to worship him, but he knew it would not come to that because people feared death deeply, especially on this damned day. Of course, some were antagonistic, some submitted reluctantly. See how it all unfolds.

Shirley landed on top of the curtain wall of the city Pygmy was destroying, she listened to the screams of terror and the shrieks. There were two enormous vantablack swords mercilessly reigning down the populace. Pygmy was darting around the city slitting the throats of those the swords were missing one by one. They barely spotted him, he would appear, slit, then disappear as quick as he had appeared.

She sat down and tried not to think about that thing that disturbed her. She could hear him laughing maniacally from up there, the laugh darted around the city, sometimes it was so loud, sometimes distant, sometimes she could not hear it at all. There were too many noises climbing over each other. She wished she could imitate that laugh. She thought she would ask him to teach her, she could use her tech to record and imitate the laugh in a woman's voice, her voice to be specific, it was odd why she did not just copy and paste it.

Pygmy slightly miscalculated his teleportation landing, he appeared beside an elderly man staring blankly in the middle of the road as the buildings fell and crushed those running around to escape the vantablack swords. He seemed absent, his glasses were cracked and foggy. He was very old, probably around 90. He was one of the few, young and old, who were diagnosed with schizophrenia at the start of the Sentinels' supposed utopia. "Few" was the word used in the media, it was a cover-up, Athanasy and Yoddha were the ones handling that situation.

He was your typical geriatric case, his body had quit on him half a decade ago, but it seemed Death was in no rush to take him, despite him lamenting and longing for death. He was walking around in his soggy, stained diaper, his gown wavered aggressively, something saturated with yellow ran down his legs while something brown, scalding, and heavy sagged his diaper. He was lumbering in the street, without a care of the chaos in the background.

Pygmy missed him with edge of his blade, he turned and swung to correct his error. He loved the looks on some of their faces just before he kills them, that look in a split of a second they would sometimes flash. Sometimes he was just too quick or distracted to see it, Shirley started believing they all showed those faces from the time when Molahlehi kidnapped three and brought them to a remote area in the middle of nowhere to show her and Pygmy.

They had missed it on the first one Molahlehi killed, Shirley saw it on the second one, and Pygmy on the third one. It was inconclusive, but they could not kidnap more from the cities. Stomper's depraved proclivity made it easy for Molahlehi to snatch three people and leave with them.

Pygmy loved those last-moment faces, they were like gold stars on his test, they made him proud of his work, he might even dream of those faces. The same face Amanirenas saw on the kid with the ice cream cone just before the toxic gas cylinder hit the ground. It was easier to see in little kids and old people than in adults.

Pygmy's jaw dropped open in a wide grin when he saw that look on the old man's face when the blade of his stunted sword slit his jugular vein, but the faces appeared for a split second. The old man's appeared and remained even after Pygmy disappeared and the old man fell to the ground and bled out.

Shirley had timed his attack from the moment she sat at the top of the curtain wall. The gigantic vantablack swords disappeared, the mixture of human and non-human sounds ceased. It took four minutes, but it took an extra nine minutes for Pygmy to appear at the top beside her. He was cleaning up the leftovers. Unfortunately, Shirley did not hear their grunts as Pygmy flashed past them. She had a weird kink of sounds people made, they made her spine tingle.

Pygmy was panting, his adrenalin rush was too much, those faces, they made his heart pulsate and his maniacal laugh more sinister. He could barely sit still for a moment, he was lightly bouncing off his heels. Shirley also noticed his hands were trembling, he wanted more. There were still more cities to massacre. She did not tell him about the thing that bothered her, she could not get it out of her mind, but she had managed to for a while.

She embraced him tightly and whispered in his ear to take deep breaths with her, his vigorous trembling slowed down on the twelfth slow breath. It had not entirely ceased, but Shirley decided he was calm enough. She gently held his hands and kissed them, then kissed his forehead, the wide grin was less stretched.

'Yes, he is better.' Shirley thought. On their way to the next city, taking their sweet precious time, she told him all about Stomper and Athanasy, but did not mention Amanirenas.

A couple of dead cities away from them, there was a damp soil that started bulging as though it were breathing. It was bobbing like the chest rising and falling as one breathed. Then, the bulge grew bigger and bigger until a hand dramatically protruded like a zombie about to come out of its grave. The hand then quickly started digging out the damp soil, another arm appeared, then they started digging themselves out of the grave.

A woman jumped out huffing, she crawled out of the shallow grave and rolled over to the side. She could still feel Stomper's hand around her neck, it gave her PTSD. Her head was pounding, it made her nose bleed. The excruciating crush still lingered. Athanasy's body was covered in grime. She was bare, in the wild.

She did not look like Athanasy, she was more human, but you could tell from a glance that she was her, like a memory of who she used to be. She was back to her old self, free from Anathema. Though, free, she had lost all her powers, even the realistic psychic abilities she had before Anathema. She had come up with this contingency plan after the terrifying discovery of Stomper's power.

She was stark bald, she did not even have eyebrows. Her skin was caramel. What she had not anticipated with this trick was the side effects, she was rendered partly blind. She could barely see, she glaumed into the damp soil for something, and pulled out a stone with a foreign symbol inscribed on it. She continued searching and pulled out a messenger bag with clothes inside. She was vulnerable in the outside, no powers, impaired sight, no weapons.

She did not make an effort or tend to the grime on her body, she just put the clothes on with it pasted all over her. Inside the messenger bag were also three culture tubes with blood samples from her previous form. She hoped drinking them might help her get her powers back. There was also a small notebook in there. She started walking. *Pew*. She suddenly fell, there was a hole on her forehead. Blood drew a trail down her face. One of Shirley's drones had gotten her. A drone Shirley had forgotten about, a drone that's been lingering around that spot for weeks because Molahlehi had told her it had to be there – now it made sense why.

Pygmy and Shirley came across an old temple, they figured they should explore it before continuing. They weren't in any hurry. "We haven't seen any of those mutated animals on our way here," Pygmy said. Shirley replied with an absent 'Yeah' as they entered the temple, it was old and broken inside. Someone entered after them, panting loudly. They both turned at the same time and saw The Jackal standing at the entrance. His eyes were ravenous, his smile malicious. "I have found you!" He said excitedly.

Pygmy applauded sarcastically and jovially congratulated him, he spoke in a voice you would hear in a show that featured an obstacle course, a dramatic excited voice of a host phrasing sentences in a way that made it seem like the contestants might die. "He'd found them both. He has not felt so proud in his life since sixth grade when his teacher told him he did a great job cleaning the whiteboard, thus he celebrates as though finding them meant he will get a treat from his disapproving master." He made funny gestures throughout the mockery. The Jackal bared his teeth and growled at Pygmy.

CHAPTER 15
WEAPONS OF A BLADE CLASH TOGETHER

The impact from the dagger and the machete expectedly led to the dagger getting knocked away from Pygmy's hand. He hopped to dodge The Jackal's foot sweep then threw a kick, but The Jackal blocked it with his forearm, so Pygmy used his forearm to launch himself away. The Jackal saw an opportunity to chase and attack him while he was in mid-air.

Pygmy threw the other dagger at The Jackal to slow him down, The Jackal effortlessly deflected it with his machete. Pygmy kicked his iklwa with a bicycle kick at The Jackal, The Jackal deflected it — there were embers. Pygmy reached the ground continued with his motion as he slid on his shins facing away from The Jackal, he arched his back backward and threw his axe at The Jackal, it sliced past The Jackal's calf. Pygmy was pleased, he opened his arms and giggled.

The damage was minor, The Jackal pulled out a second machete and charged at Pygmy, Pygmy took out both short swords and twisted his body to face The Jackal as he hopped to get on his feet. Then he, too, charged at The Jackal. Shirley observed them fighting, their movements were immaculate, and flitting. She was recording them with her lens. It was a fun fight to witness, she envied them, she wanted to join in.

The Jackal thrusted his machete at Pygmy, Pygmy dodged but it grazed his right cheek, while The Jackal's arm was still extended, Pygmy hastened and twirled as he swung his sword to cut The Jackal's wrist, but the Jackal was agile enough to withdraw his arm on time, he did not waste time, he quickly swung the other arm to cut Pygmy as he had slyly lured him in.

To his surprise, Pygmy did not attempt to retreat, he thrusted the butt of his sword handle against The Jackal's bicep, which halted The Jackal's arm, then shoved his barbed wire vambrace across The Jackal's chest, but The Jackal saved himself in the nick of time with a swift upward kick. Pygmy disappeared before it could get him. He re-appeared farther away before The Jackal.

The Jackal contracted and relaxed his bicep repeatedly until he noticed that Pygmy was holding one short sword and the axe. He gasped as he recoiled at the last millisecond, the other short sword was projected from above and almost stabbed his head, he was briefly on edge with how fast Pygmy was, then his edge turned into ire when he realized Pygmy was being frivolous from the moment they started fighting.

He yelled at Pygmy with froth in his mouth, "You! You think this is a game? Keep playing, it makes it easier for me to decapitate you and bring your head back home with me! *Both* your heads!" He pulled out his trench knives from his sides, Pygmy applauded jovially. The two machetes slowly turned invisible as they floated in the air behind The Jackal's shoulders, this made Pygmy stop applauding, he was not familiar with this technique, he did not have such a technique in his arsenal.

The Jackal found pleasure in seeing Pygmy look less frivolous and more uneasy, he grinned at him and told him, "I believe you do not have such techniques, how pathetic."

Shirley called Pygmy, "Preence, I cannot see his machetes, but I can track them by following their energy fields. I will borrow you my lens-" The Jackal shifted his attention to Shirley and with a mad look on his face exclaimed, "Die!"

One of the invisible machetes shot at Shirley, Pygmy lunged to The Jackal, nigh too quick for The Jackal, it was as though he had teleported, he was in motion swinging his axe at The Jackal's chest, unfortunately for him, The Jackal could now better keep up with his flit movements.

There was a loud clang and sparks between the axe and an invisible force guarding The Jackal's chest, it was the invisible machete. At the same time the other projected machete missed Shirley and stabbed into the wall, she had narrowly escaped as it had caught her off guard with The Jackal's sudden upheaval of speed. Two explosions went off from both machetes.

The force of the explosions made Shirley lurch even though she had flown high up. She smiled with relief when she saw Pygmy out of reach of the wildfires, he had evaded the explosion and gathered all his weapons.

He looked up at Shirley and asked her to leave the temple and to keep her eye on the other machete that was trying to kill her, as her presence there ma—

The Jackal had precipitously appeared before Pygmy with his right arm extended at him, Pygmy was caught off guard, but he was quicker than The Jackal, at least he believed he was. He managed to block the trench knife with both his iklwa and axe, but at the immediate moment of contact, there was another explosion, this time it blew Pygmy through the wall of the door of the temple and he was projected outside the temple. He thought the explosions came only from the machetes' direct contact, but he was mistaken.

Shirley cried, "Preence!" and hurried down to him, forgetting about the machete that was stalking her. She found him on the steps, smoke was emanating from his body, he was getting up from the ground and groaning, she landed beside him and helped him up — he was burning up. She advised him, "Now might be a good time to use one of *your* techniques,"

He snorted a laugh and replied, "Where's the fun in that?" She sighed, he was playing a dangerous game. She offered to give him her lens to spot the invisible machetes but he refused. He put the handle of the axe between his upper and lower teeth, he held the iklwa on the left and one short sword on the right and stuck the daggers into his hair.

He said in a muffled voice, "Watch me take him down in base form."

"How, when you can't even see his machetes?" She asked angrily. Pygmy shrugged casually and laughed. The Jackal walked out of the temple with a smirk. Neither the fires nor the force of the explosions affected him. Pygmy instructed Shirley not to interfere, she contended but he instantly disappeared and appeared before The Jackal.

He had crouched, he swung the axe with his teeth at The Jackal's knee, The Jackal hopped back to elude, Pygmy almost had him, then, the clang again, then an explosion swallowed him. Shirley gasped, she did not catch if Pygmy disappeared before the explosion or not, but she did spot the lingering energy of the machete, there was just not enough time to warn him. Not that he would have wanted her to warn him. She breathed a sigh of relief when she heard his maniac laughter.

He appeared behind The Jackal, swinging his sword down at his shoulder, The Jackal blocked it with his trench knife, another explosion. Pygmy appeared beside Shirley and instantaneously disappeared before she could turn her head, but she had caught a whiff of the strong smell of fire.

Pygmy shot through the flames, The Jackal blocked, another explosion, he disappeared at the last millisecond, then briefly waited before he attacked again, not waiting for the flames to die out. This went on around 8 or 9 times, each consecutive explosion fueled the flames of the previous explosion — there was an enormous amalgam of fire that reached the temple and blew it away, it even forced Shirley to back away farther. Shirley was not sure of what Pygmy was planning.

Pygmy managed to discern that the flames did not affect The Jackal's sight at all, he could see clearly through the fire and the excess smoke. He suddenly popped up before The Jackal, The Jackal was in a poised stance, he saw him coming.

The Jackal was stunned at the sight, Pygmy was engulfed in flames, but he had a wide mouth that produced a maniacal laugh, he seemed to be enjoying this fight, despite the fire burning him. But another thing that worried The Jackal was the missing weapons, Pygmy only held the axe in his hand.

He swung the axe at The Jackal, as expected, The Jackal kept up and blocked it, but at the pending moment of collision, Pygmy adjusted his arm to miss The Jackal's trench knives, the irregular abrupt change in motion snapped some of Pygmy's bones, he retreated that arm and used the other arm he was hiding behind his back to throw a dagger at The Jackal's abdomen. The clang of the machete was a bit late, it scratched the hilt of the dagger, but the dagger managed to stab The Jackal's abdomen. Before the explosion, there were multiple squelching noises that were masked by the sound of the explosion.

Pygmy appeared beside Shirley, he had narrowly escaped on time but the force of the explosion continued his inertia and he shot down the steps. Shirley zoomed to him, he was covered in smoke and small fires.

She caught him, he was scalding to the touch, she extinguished the fires, there was sizzling. He couldn't stand upright yet, he huffed and laughed. "I told you I can take him down without using my techniques."

Once her vision from the steam was clear, she gasped at the sight, he was covered in second degree burns, but he had a third degree burn on the left side of his face, but he was nonetheless mirthful. They both turned at the harrowing screams of anger of The Jackal standing at the top of the steps in a particular posture to indicate the unbearable pain he was in. Shirley saw the end result of Pygmy's masochistic plan.

A dagger through The Jackal's abdomen, another through his thigh, the axe planted on the left side of his neck - punctured his jugular vein, a short sword through the side of his rib cage, the other one through his groin. The iklwa was missing, but it had taken out his right eye, Pygmy had intended to shove it into his head.

Shirley deduced that those ephemeral moments after the explosions, Pygmy was not letting the fires settle a bit before striking again, he was appearing at distant calculated areas and hurling his weapons at The Jackal while he continuously distracted him with the attacks so he does not catch up to his plan.

'Quite shrewd.' Shirley thought to herself, she was impressed. The Jackal was bleeding excessively. Shirley urgently asked Pygmy if he could stand up, he asked her why, since The Jackal was obviously done for. She had an extremely worried look on her face, she told him, "Because we are surrounded by hundreds of exploding weapons, ranging for approximately 70 meters!"

She looked up at The Jackal with an agitated look on her face, Pygmy was confounded, but he figured Shirley was devising a plan she did not tell him about. The Jackal was going to take them out with him, since his fate was already sealed. He grinned, his teeth red as blood poured out of his mouth. He made the weapons touch each other, there was an explosion that shook the heavens.

Despite The Jackal not being affected by the explosion, the force affected Pygmy's weapons, the dagger in the abdomen shot through and pierced his spinal cord which made him collapse, the one in the groin made him gush out blood as it went through as well, the one in his rib cage sliced his lung, the dagger in his thigh got lodged in deeper, the axe (which was keeping blood from gushing out) was blown away, the blood squirted. He died from excess bleeding.

Pygmy watched the explosion from afar as it darkened the sky, what a splendor way to go out. He waited for the explosion to cease, then he teleported back to the scene. The mutated animals that did not run away during the first successive explosions got caught in the massive one.

The heat from that spot made his burn marks hiss and sting, but he ignored it, he was in a hole of endless glasses, the fire was hot enough to turn the sand into glass. There were still fires in most parts of the area. He peered around for Shirley, he was quickly getting worried because the dark smoke blinded him from seeing her, with his now blurry left eye it was harder to see.

He saw Shirley's ball of force field gleaming in the darkness and rushed to it. He wiped the ash off its surface and was greeted with a blush and a wave from Shirley. He was relieved, he smiled and waved back. He sat on the glass ground and leaned against the shield.

He chuckled and told her, "That was fun, wasn't it?"

She scoffed and responded, "You could have avoided taking that much damage if you had used at least one technique," he waved off casually and asked, "Where's the fun in that?" Shirley remained in the shield because the lingering effects of such an explosion would affect her, because she was just an intelligent human being, not a part human with god-like power. Although, the heat was affecting Pygmy, it did not incapacitate him.

He enquired, "Hey, why'd you make The Jackal think he had won before he croaked?"

She responded, "So he "croaks" with confidence, not miserably and feeling like a complete failure."

"He doesn't deserve such mercy. I was going to laugh at his face and mock him before teleporting away."

"I know, but he probably thought you could get away and I'd be left behind. Guess he discerned that you cannot teleport others away with you. If there's any afterlife for those with Anathema's power, at least he'd rest easy and proud of himself."

Pygmy jerked up and exclaimed, "Loophole!" He elaborated, "When we kill the rest of the Sentinels, they will break his false sense of accomplishment. I'd love to see that."

Shirley sighed. "I guess. At least I tried to help,"

It was quiet for a while, except for the raging fire, then Pygmy asked, "Hey, notice how The Jackal's fire is similar to a variation of Molahlehi's?"

Shirley paused to think about it, if Pygmy was right, then that would suggest that Molahlehi might also have a fraction of Anathema's power. Neither of them knew of Molahlehi's history. Pygmy sighed and said with disappointment, "Now, you have to go to the farthest remaining cities and wreak havoc, I will attack the near cities to lure out the Sentinels. I wish I could come with you,"

Shirley laughed. "I don't need to be babysat, you know. I raised you and taught you how to read. It's time to grow up, now. This world doesn't deserve such fragile emotions." Pygmy looked at her with visible confusion, she was partially contradicting herself.

Before parting ways, Shirley hugged Pygmy tightly. It was a different hug from the usual light, affectionate hugs. Pygmy did not know what it meant, it must have had something to do with her thinking she would die on this mission, but it was the kind of hug that someone gives someone they never want to let go. She was profoundly fond of him. Maybe she feared *he* would die.

After the hug, she pinched Pygmy's cheeks and told him, "Please be safe. I *love* you so much, Preence, more than you can ever imagine, and I care deeply for you." She hovered her hand around the third degree burn and remarked, "We have to do something about the side of your face."

Another thing that confused Pygmy was how she pronounced the word 'love', Pygmy had never seen Shirley afraid, so he figured this was her being afraid. He hugged her and told her to be safe, too, and that he also loved her and cared deeply for her. After the hug, she reminded him of the surprise she mentioned. Pygmy was intrigued, but she zipped her lips and told him she would reveal it to him when they meet again.

She remembered one more thing; "Please don't worry if you do not hear from me, I don't want you to be distracted on your mission. Remember, I'm the older one, so I know more than you do, so I will survive — then I'll call you."

CHAPTER 16
THE TRUTH OF IT ALL

By the time Yoddha's strange, morphed creature reached the city, Stomper had already proclaimed himself the cities' sole deity, and had murdered and put on display those who had refused to bow down to him, but this was not the city Stomper had passed by, it was a city Shirley had passed by. Yoddha stopped his weird centipede ride and hopped onto the curtain wall, he walked over the wall with a feeling of unease, he could never beat Stomper, especially if he really is in cahoots with those two.

Everyone within the curtain wall was charred. They all died where they were standing and just remained in those black statues as though an exhibition at a museum, a very disconcerting exhibition. He was appalled. He could not make sense of this, it did not make any sense, the buildings were intact, what kind of explosion does this?

If it was even an explosion, those charred corpses wouldn't be as they were, they would have been blown away by the explosion. Yoddha quickly concluded this was the man with the white hair's doing, he was the one with the fire. It seemed everything Athanasy had said was true, Stomper and these two monsters were—

The explosion of The Jackal's final trick shook the curtain wall around the city and caused a worrying seismic activity that caused his hair and cloak to flutter aggressively to the strong gales of the explosions. He saw the explosion from that distance, it was impossible to miss.

So Athanasy and Amanirenas were dead, Stomper was unhinged, Bullpit was MIA, The Jackal might be dead or alive. He seemed to be the remaining pillar of the Sentinels, if he wanted to keep breathing, he deduced the best option would be to join Stomper and his two accomplices. Then, perhaps over time he could devise a plan to take them down, he was fairly smarter than Stomper.

He stared down at the city with pity (as Molahlehi had at Pygmy and Shirley), how those people did not expect the attack. They were caught off guard. They probably thought it would be another normal day, just going about their daily routines. If they were to turn into ghosts, they would be those ghosts that were not aware they were dead.

They would be in denial to the fact that those black sculptures in their cities were their corpses. Obviously what that kid with the malicious grin did was fleeting, if it were not, then some of the corpses' body language would suggest they were in distress – Yoddha believed. More of his black mass percolated through the back of the cloak and molded into wings, he flapped them and flew down to the city, another black mass crawled across his face, covering his nose and mouth, protecting him from breathing in anything he should not inhale.

He landed on the highway, the vehicles were all burned, the unsuspecting charred bodies were stuck stirring their wheels. There had been multiple accidents, when whatever the man with the white hair did hit – now Yoddha believed it was Molahlehi – some vehicles had skidded off the track and crashed into other vehicles coming from the opposite direction. There was a semi-truck that had driven off the road and crashed into a house.

There was a tanker truck, its tank had caught fire and caused an explosion that caused the bridge to collapse and wipe out everything that was near that road. All that was left was a trail of black on the tar and a couple of small pieces of the tank strewn on the road.

On the ground, on the side of the road next to the collapsed bridge was another burned black sculpture of a man with what seemed to be a toddler, they were extra cooked – something you'd think Stomper would like, but he'd once said cooked humans were like contraceptives, and he did not like contraceptives. Yoddha continued flying around the city searchingly, he was hoping to find some survivors. He entered houses, buildings, a few cellars, it seemed everyone was killed by the attack, no one was spared. But what kind of an attack reaches people everywhere without breaking down their doors? This scared Yoddha. All the gas stations were blown to bits.

Another thing that Yoddha discovered was that all the water was boiling hot. He could not bear watching any more charred sculptures of horror. He prayed for them and flew out of the city and made his way to a city near that widespread explosion, he believed he might arrive not too late and manage to stop another city from falling victim to these sick people's deeds.

Whoever he finds, he would negotiate with them to spare the people and offer to join them, he wondered if Stomper was the leader, but of course he was, he *had* to be the leader, the kid with the malicious grin was not the leader — Stomper would not stand for that. He had once laughed hysterically when Athanasy volunteered to be the Sentinels' leader, he did not like being told what to do.

Neither of Stomper's parents ever let him do what he wanted when he was young, so now he ensures everyone doesn't do what they want without his permission, if and only if whatever they do does not displease him – that was even more true with what he was doing in the cities. Yoddha used such thoughts to keep his mind busy as he rode his creature to the city he hoped to prevent from perishing.

The gloomy smoke from The Jackal's trick was not dissipating, it lingered in a vast distance. Looking at it made Shirley uncomfortable, it looked and felt like something from a horror movie, like if you get inside that smoke your worst nightmares come to life and do unspeakable things to you. She had sent a drone into that foggy nightmare, there was nothing scary in there, she and Pygmy had been inside it before parting, she felt silly for worrying.

She was standing on the curtain wall of the same city Yoddha was hurrying toward, she turned away from the smoke and to the city, there was a carnival. You could taste the fun in the air and feel the people's laughter on your skin, this made her retch.

There was a slideshow of Amanirenas and Athanasy's pictures on the jumbotrons, the mayor of this city was part of the mayors who did not stick around to watch the entire livestream of Stomper, the city had cut off communication with the other cities for the sake of pacifying the petrified civilians, so they also were oblivious to Stomper's new endeavor. People needed something to take their mind off Stomper, if things were to go to the dump, then they'd spend those last moments being happy.

Shirley did not feel bad for them, at least not in the way you'd think. Like how she knew the reason those people charged at Stomper knowing they would die. She believed some, despite the hard truth of what they knew was happening, did not have the courage to do it. No, they were too repressed, they did not have enough willpower. She knew they could not commit suicide even if they wanted to, charging at Stomper was an indirect suicide. At least, this correlated with the faces. They wanted the same thing.

She loved the lights, the scene was beautiful, if she did not know the harsh reality of what happened 16 years ago, she would spare these people. But she knew, and they had to die, every last one of them. She was almost out of ammo. The monitor on her left arm pinged, she fiddled with it and saw in one of the nine drones that lingered miles around the city to spot any incoming threat. The motion sensors were going crazy, she saw what the camera saw, it was Yoddha on his strange centipede monster heading toward the city.

She was aware that ordinary fire could not hurt the Sentinels, for some reason, this crucial information came from Molahlehi. So, blowing Yoddha up would not help, but chopping him up into tiny bits might work, maybe she could use her laser to turn his body to a plural. She had a better idea, she deployed her nanobots. She would not attack him, she sat down and watched the people down there enjoy the carnival, she was not threatened by Yoddha.

When Yoddha was nearing the city she shot tranquilizers into the heavily armed guards outside the gates who were waiting for Stomper to show up so they could show him hell. She gave Yoddha a sign by shooting her laser to the ground outside the wall, Yoddha was bemused at first. Whatever or whoever it was, wanted his attention, and they got it, he was relieved he would negotiate with... He realized it was neither of the people he thought he would negotiate with. He put his guard up.

He landed on the curtain wall beside her, she was sitting down without a care for him, watching those people with a disgusted look in her eyes. Yoddha questioned her, he asked her what and who she was, if she worked with Stomper and those two, if she was responsible for the annihilation of the city he had just come from, and if she was the one who had caused that far away explosion.

"You ask a lot of questions, Yoddha, you know that?" She said. He wanted to ask how she knew his name, but that did not seem relevant, he repeated his questions with lesser patience.

"Who I am is none of your business. I am working with "the white-haired man" and "the kid with the malicious grin", but we're not working with Stomper. You actually bought what Athanasy said? I thought you were the smartest of the Sentinels." She replied.

Yoddha took a step forward, he said with hostility, "Then, what are you doing here and what do you want? Your friend with the white hair nearly killed me."

"Nearly. Didn't. That was intentional. I'm guessing if you're here, Athanasy is dead, Amanirenas is somewhere out there, Stomper is chasing a dream I will personally destroy, and The Jackal is dead, then Bullpit is the one you sent after Molahlehi."

"What are you talking about? Who's Molahlehi? If Athanasy was lying then who killed The Jackal? Why didn't your friend kill me? Where's the other one, the one with the malicious grin?"

"You really do ask a lot of questions. Let me catch you up to speed. Amanirenas is alive, I spared her life and it bothers me that I did – I had forgotten about it – great! Thanks a lot! The Jackal just died a while ago, you see that smoke? The one with the malicious grin, his name is Pygmy to you, he killed The Jackal. Molahlehi is the one with white hair, he spared you because he wanted you to suffer. We are going to destroy everything you've all built, then, one by one, we will kill you all."

Yoddha scoffed and said derisively, "I don't believe you. And you can't kill Stomper, no one can kill Stomper. *Nothing* can kill Stomper. And I won't let you kill these people," he paused, and asked, "Are you the one responsible for murdering all those people in the ninth city?"

Shirley grunted, she was annoyed by all his questions. She stood up and faced him, she responded, "I honestly don't give a shit if you believe me or not. What city are you referring to? I've destroyed so many today." Her response and the way she responded like murdering hundreds of thousands was something like a house chore or something insignificant.

His black mass extended from under his cloak under his left arm and formed an urumi, its blades accumulated on the ground. The giant centipede monster started tweaking. Four thick red dots whose source was unknown appeared on Yoddha's chest. Two more armed drones appeared between Yoddha and Shirley. Her laser also activated and pointed at his forehead.

She sighed and said wearily, "We are going to fight, I might die. I'm only human, you're sort of a god. From what I know, only Athanasy knows what those things you call humans are, that's why she plays with their lives." She said, "You never bothered to ask why we kill these "people" in cold blood." She air-quoted.

She made it clear; "We are still going to fight, and I'm still going to turn all those laughs down there into shrieks and those bright colors into red. But I guess you deserve to know the truth." Yoddha scoffed and formed another urumi on the other hand. But he started coughing and sneezing, as if dust motes were gathering around his face. His eyes were momentarily watery, Shirley let it subside, then, she told him the truth.

16 years ago, when the Sentinels of Anathema came to be, Anathema did not only decide his payment for their powers be paid by the millions of people in this small world, he also did something else, something that stayed between him and Athanasy. He possessed every single remaining human, but the downside of his presence lurking inside them was that it overwhelmed and killed them.

So, all those people in all those cities are actually dead, they are actually Anathema. The only thing keeping their souls from departing from their bodies is Anathema's presence because if their souls leave their bodies he would perish. The people are trapped inside their own minds, suffering every single day in an endless torturous loop as Anathema feeds on their infinite souls and pain.

They are forced to believe they are still alive, that the decisions they make and the lives they live are theirs. Subconsciously they know Anathema manipulates them and is actually making these decisions and lives their lives. Pygmy and Shirley never understood why he does this, they believed it was because he craved life, that he craved being human and living a normal human life. But those people were suffering, and they were trapped. From the three that Molahlehi had kidnapped, they had concluded that those people had died moments after Anathema inhabited their bodies and infested their minds, so even if Pygmy, Molahlehi, and Shirley could force Anathema out of their bodies, all that would remain would be dead bodies.

When those people charged at Stomper after he blew up Athanasy's blob knowing they would die, they were doing so so that they could be free. As none of them could commit suicide, that moment when they gained enough willpower over Anathema and charge at Stomper, it was similar to moments before they die, the faces they made.

Those peaceful faces they made before death, they were happy to be free. Seeing them welcome death so they could escape Anathema's torment was the gold star in Pygmy's work, it was the main reason they were doing all they were doing. That, and getting revenge on the Sentinels for bringing in this abhorrent evil into their world and taking away their loved ones, avenging all those who died because of these so-called Sentinels' lust for power.

The story of them summoning Anathema to stop the sky from bleeding leeches and that whole Mother Nature story was bull. He had crept into this world after they summoned him and wreaked havoc, they did not remember much from those moments when Anathema was summoned, but him giving them these powers was tied to him taking sacrifices of the millions who survived the sky leeches and sparing just over five hundred thousand people.

Those who were diagnosed with schizophrenia at the beginning of the building of the 35 cities were those whose minds utterly rejected Anathema's presence, and him forcibly opposing their minds led to their poor minds shattering. He still lingered inside their minds, perhaps he wanted the full human experience, the good and the bad.

Of course, Yoddha did not believe her, he laughed it off as a lie. He entertained her, and inquired, "If this poorly assembled lie of yours is true, then what? You're going to kill every single human left and leave the world as it is? Or are you going to mate, the three of you, and rebuild society via incest? What's your endgame?"

Shirley smiled, she did not care if he believed her or not, she iterated that she did not care if he believed her or not. But that was not why she smiled, she had gotten him. His fate was sealed, she figured if she was going to kill him anyway, she should tell him the rest. This was similar to what she was trying to do for The Jackal and what she did for Amanirenas.

She revealed to him; "We have a secret underground facility with 500 people. Each genetically unique. Groups from all the races and as many cultures that exist in the world. None related to each other. We put them in capsules, they are comatose, but once we're done with this mission, they will rebuild this world. We live in a very small world, so it's possible. I mean, if you've read the Bible and how everything started, you could say 500 people is more than enough."

Yoddha's nose bled, he wiped it dismissively and asked her suspiciously, "If that's all true, then why are you telling me? I will kill you and go let Stomper know of your plan."

She got into a stance as more drones appeared, she tapped on the monitor, watched for a few seconds, then laughed a laugh that was an emulation of Pygmy's and told him with a smug, "You're not making it out alive from this. You can kill me, but my mission is complete."

Yoddha's monster began rising as it grew larger and larger, he responded looking at her with disdain, "A couple of drones aren't enough to kill me or my counterpart. I'm going to stop you from accomplishing whatever mission you speak of. You shouldn't have revealed all—" he coughed.

Shirley revealed one last thing with that similar maniacal look on her face that Pygmy has; "The drones aren't for you, they are for your "counterpart" and my mission is already complete. I have destroyed the remaining cities. All of them. Inside you are hundreds of nanobots, don't bother trying to vomit or use your black mass. They are dismantling your DNA, picking it apart. So you're going to die shortly, but that gives you enough time to fight me and kill me. And as for this city, it is also done for. I have planted the same radiation device from the city you just came from. It should go off any second now."

Before the messy fight began, she murmured distantly under her breath, "I love you, Preence, more than you can ever imagine,"

CHAPTER 17
SHIVERS

Amanirenas woke up to a bunch of bird-like creatures trying to tug her heavy body, it made sense that they could not drag her as she weighed just over 200 kilograms – all muscles. Their beaks were pinching her skin and her scalp when they tried dragging her using her hair.

When she woke up, they screeched and scattered. She was in a creek. She had a distant migraine that was indecisive of whether it would stay or leave. She remembered the acidic taste of the toxic gas, she believed it may have done modicum damage to her lungs, but she was a Sentinel, she would heal. Getting up was very difficult, but she managed to, until her knees gave in when she remembered all those people she could not save, the look on that kid's face before the toxic gas cylinder hit the ground.

Unlike when that man found her on the roof, she did not need to hide her weeping. There was no one out here to ask her why she was crying, or look at her with fear of what could make such a superhuman break down and weep. The sun's rays were permeating through the small openings of the trees over her. She sat there, tears pouring out of her eyes endlessly.

Then, she realized, this was her way out, she had been looking for a way out and this was it. She hoped no one saw her escape the toxic gas, and judging from the few blisters and a splotch of first degree burn on her arm, everyone was most likely vaporized.

Those who had been watching might even assume she had died, that was good, she would keep it that way. She was tired of the Sentinels of Anathema life. She made a decision, she stood up again, this time she did not collapse. She began walking, she would search for Pygmy and Molahlehi, and offer a team-up to take down Stomper. He had to go.

Molahlehi was sitting on top of the shade structure of a taxi rank in a side-sitting position, but the taxis were no longer functioning and there was grass everywhere. He had tied his dreads back in a ponytail with none whatsoever over his face, he wore his mokorotlo straight this time, his blankets were always almost as long as cloaks. He had formed a flower using his fire.

He heard a wreckage that caused light quakes, he adjusted his focus from the flower to the thing beyond, the thing that was causing such reverberations. It was a figure skipping over large distances, heading toward him. The figure landed a couple of blocks from Molahlehi, but the strong seismic activity reached him. The figure skipped one last time, it became visible in the sky — it was Bullpit, and he was going to land on Molahlehi.

Molahlehi looked up at him nonchalantly, then, Bullpit was engulfed by a fire as he was reaching his maximum height. Molahlehi stood up and hopped out of the way, landing on a T-junction between what used to be two butcheries. He briefly admired how Bullpit in that fire resembled a meteor.

Bullpit landed and an explosion went off. Bullpit shot through the ground, the already inactive vehicles got caught in the fire. Molahlehi jeered and turned around to walk, but the sudden wind that blew as Bullpit catapulted to him made him stop, Bullpit was about to grab his hair and probably yank him, but Molahlehi effortlessly tipped over to the side, twirled and planted his fist on Bullpit's chest. He was impressed of how resistant Bullpit's clothes were to his fire, he was also intrigued of how far Bullpit's invulnerability extended.

The punch did not hurt Bullpit that much, his clapped his hands to crush Molahlehi, but Molahlehi had abruptly turned into smoke. He appeared beside Bullpit standing casually, facing the front and not glancing at Bullpit, Bullpit adjusted his motion and attacked him, but was suddenly blown away by a big circle that stood between Molahlehi and him, beaming very wild fire that bellowed. The fire beam destroyed everything in its path, even burning away the tar and leaving not a single trace of anything it touched. Unlike fire which releases heat in the vicinity, this one was laser-focused and all that wasted energy was crumbled inside the beam, and it did not leave smoke as an after-effect. The vehicles that weren't entirely caught by the beam had clean cuts with smoldering fires at the edges of the cuts.

Molahlehi could not spot Bullpit, but he could sense him, somewhere. He patiently waited for Bullpit to crawl out of the ground at the end of the beam, this was becoming interesting for him. He urged Bullpit, "Come on, now. Crawl out already. You're not dead yet, that wasn't enough to kill you."

There was movement underneath the smoldering ground, Bullpit's arm reached out, he steadily emerged. Molahlehi smiled to himself. Bullpit was buck naked, that variant of Molahlehi's fire managed to burn the durable material Athanasy had made for Bullpit. Molahlehi burned away his clothes to humiliate him, but being naked did not seem to make Bullpit ashamed. He glowered at Molahlehi. Molahlehi reached out his hand and beckoned him.

Bullpit bolted to him, Molahlehi did not move or get into a stance until the very last moment, then something snatched Bullpit out of his way, the speed that Bullpit and this thing collided caused them to project to separate routes, they both crashed into different stores.

Bullpit burst out of the store angered by Molahlehi's persistent nonchalance that hindered him from landing a blow on him. He gnarled at whatever snatched him; he was going to tear it to shreds. A dragon emerged, but it didn't have wings, it had a muscular build, it was five feet tall, it looked like a hell hound, but its scales and dragon-centric face gave away the reptilian characteristics. Bullpit was not sure such a dragon ever existed, it was definitely not a drake dragon.

"Like it? I created it myself. It's not difficult, I just stuff a certain amount of my differing fires in different bodies and link those bodies with my consciousness," Molahlehi began, then asked, "Sound familiar?" It tackled Bullpit, he did not back down, Molahlehi watched him wrestle with the dragon. It was very aggressive wrestling. Molahlehi despised every single member of the Sentinels, for he knew their darkest secret, he was the one who had relayed that information to Pygmy and Shirley, which made them despise the Sentinels, as well.

The dragon was on top of Bullpit trying to scratch him with its claws and bite him, but its gnawing attempts at his forearm shattered its teeth, and its claws snapped off when it tried to claw his face, Bullpit kicked it off him and shut its mouth before it could spew fire at him. He pounded its head with his fist, he deformed its head until it stopped moving. He was tired of the games. He began charging at Molahlehi. Molahlehi began morphing and taking up a bestial appearance, he was changing into another variant of his innovative dragons. The transformation was haste as Bullpit approached at rapid speed.

This dragon variant resembled a centaur, with majestic two pairs of wings – the upper pair bigger than the lower pair. Its muzzle was thin and long. The eyes remained the same colorful eyes, its scaly skin was rose. It turned to the sky and opened its mouth to spew fire, Bullpit increased his speed. When he was close, certain he would get there on time, it turned its head down to face him, then a blue fire with green sparks shot out from its mouth and eyes.

It let out a *pew* kind of sound. Bullpit covered his face with his forearms and continued charging, when the fire hit him he felt its exponentially high heat, opposed to the previous fire. This became the first time since being granted Anathema's powers that he felt physical discomfort. He measured that The Jackal's fire was parred with the first fire that Molahlehi used on him when he was plummeting to him.

He pushed against the aggressive coercion of fire until there was a 4 feet distance between him and Molahlehi, but then he felt the fire becoming unbearably hot and its force becoming fixed and impossible to push any further, like a wall. Molahlehi abruptly reverted from his dragon form, Bullpit staggered forward and almost fell. Both his forearms were clean, not at all affected, Molahlehi loved it. Molahlehi began, "You know, the variations of my f-" Bullpit jumped at him, Molahlehi's reflexes were beyond Bullpit's impressive speed. He landed on the side of a building, Bullpit did not know how he stuck to the wall, Molahlehi beckoned him with two hands. Bullpit growled and hopped at him.

One attack after the other, Bullpit went off, but Molahlehi effortlessly dodged each attack while keeping his calm demeanor. They wrecked through some of the stores as Bullpit persisted after Molahlehi. They had run into the mutated animals' shelters and nesting grounds and the poor animals became collateral damage. Bullpit was brisk and aggressive, but Molahlehi was swift and calm. The town was being wrecked at a rapid pace.

Molahlehi landed on top of a skewed building that used to be a Home Affairs building and told Bullpit, "You have tenacity, but this is futile." Bullpit catapulted from the rubble Molahlehi had left him at, Molahlehi charged at Bullpit, too, but whisked past him and landed on the rubble as Bullpit wrecked the former Home Affairs building and continued to the sky.

Molahlehi crossed his arms under the traditional blanket and began pondering about something he could not seem to figure out, he wanted to find out through a practical experiment, but felt it would have been considerate of him to ask Bullpit first. When he came to, Bullpit's fist was right before his eyes, he widened his eyes, he was caught off guard. He could have evaded it to either side, but his dreadlocks pony tail would have been caught, and he loved his dreadlocks, so instead, he beamed Bullpit to the sky with a beam of white blinding light like a quasar. It was ephemeral that Bullpit did not see it, he merely felt a sudden burning sensation throughout his entire body and suddenly being lifted higher from the ground, and witnessed his fist going over Molahlehi's hat.

As if it could not get any worse, Molahlehi kicked him on the side with a roundhouse kick, shooting him into a far away forest. Another thing that Bullpit did not see was the hole the ephemeral white light made of fire had pierced through the ground. Poor Bullpit bounced off the ground hitting trees and boulders, he had very few lesions strewn across his body — that should have been impossible.

Molahlehi appeared before him as soon as he came to a stop and laughed. "Tenacity pays, after all, doesn't it? In all the years I have trained with Pygmy and Shirley, neither of them have ever came close to landing a blow on me. Even with Pygmy's teleportation I could see him coming. But I didn't see you coming. And I never thought I'd use that variant of fire on anyone except Stomper. You have potential,"

Bullpit attempted to catch Molahlehi by surprise again with a quick attack, but Molahlehi blocked it and hit the small of his back, rendering him immobile. He fell back to the ground. Molahlehi crouched in front of him and asked, "I have been meaning to ask, why do you let Stomper treat you the way he does when you can clearly take him on? My fourth strongest fire couldn't even burn through the surface of your skin. Is my theory correct about your insides not being as hard as your skin?"

Bullpit groaned as he struggled to speak. "You ha... a-ve been... watching... u-us?"

Molahlehi replied flatly, "I have been watching all of you before you were even born."

Bullpit lamented, "Why didn't... you, stop us then? Ba-back then?" Molahlehi could have stopped them as he knew what was coming, there were so many mysteries about Molahlehi's past. He replied, "That's none of your business. Now, I haven't been watching you 24/7 so there are things I don't know yet. So, my theory is correct? I believed that was why you never challenged him, because his space-benders cannot affect you externally, but internally, they could turn your insides to mash."

Bullpit coughed a raspy cough, and questioned him, "You used Anathema's power, didn't you?" He was fighting off the paralysis from Molahlehi hitting his pressure point, Molahlehi marveled at him, he continued, "Then you're no better than us. You paid the same price we had to pay for our powers. You're a hypocrite." His body started twitching, he was starting to move, Molahlehi sighed and shook his head. *'So much wasted potential.'* He thought to himself.

He cupped his hand and whispered comically to Bullpit, "I'm going to kill you, now. I was going to squeeze out your insides and wear your skin, then go gut Stomper, but I am having second thoughts about that," Bullpit felt shivers down his spine. Those shivers. Molahlehi snapped his neck and killed him.

CHAPTER 18
THREE IS A CROWD

Pygmy ran into Amanirenas in his idle venturing, he had been expecting the Sentinels of Anathema to send more reinforcements after The Jackal did not return, and he was elated that they sent another potential murder victim. He was walking on top of a train on an old, abandoned railway track, there was overgrown grass and a pervasive stench. He hopped to the sky so Amanirenas could see him better and come to him.

Amanirenas could not make if he was luring her in to a trap, so she proceeded with caution. She walked past a train station that was taken over by grass and some passive squealing, probably one of the creatures' litter. She continued walking. She did not want to fly as that would leave her exposed to whatever malicious plan Pygmy had.

She was fierce and powerful, she had super strength that brought Stomper discomfort. She could probably take out Pygmy on her own, but she did not want to underestimate him, she was smart, unlike The Jackal. She told herself she would not let hubris be the reason for her downfall, she believed that was a pathetic way to fall.

There were four immobile trains beyond the station, Pygmy joyfully invited her to join him on top of the second one to her left. She resented his frivolity. He was a monster, similar to her dear Bullpit, but her dear Bullpit was a lawful monster, his only offence was partaking in the ritual to summon Anathema and offering millions of lives in exchange for the power of the gods – of course, he had asked Athanasy to erase his knowledge of Stomper's depraved desires because his "moral compass" would not tolerate being silent about such things.

It did not sit well with Amanirenas, having him go after the suicide bomber, she believed these monsters were exhibiting fractions of their abilities, and strongly believed they had been studying them and their abilities. But sometimes you need monsters to kill monsters.

"Are you narrating in your mind? Are you wondering if I had set traps for you?" Pygmy asked her. She did not respond, so Pygmy hopped off the train, he landed on the railway track and began walking toward her on one rail playfully. He assured her, "There are not traps here, I don't need them to kill you, Amanirenas, or any one of the Sentinels." He stopped three feet away from her, he looked her in the eye and continued, "You're not Stomper, I'm not Molahlehi. So we—"

"I can blast through you and splatter your rotten insides everywhere and kill you right now." Amanirenas threatened him. He opened his arms and encouraged her to do that, he was overly confident in himself, Amanirenas thought. She still feared this was a trap, she did not know how many allies he had, there could be others hiding. Something might happen to her if she attempts to blast through him.

Pygmy hopped out of her way and asked to go fight somewhere she felt comfortable, this angered Amanirenas. If there weren't any traps, then how much he belittled her. No worries, his hubris will be his downfall. She led him, he followed, it started raining. She noticed that cut on his face and his burn marks that weren't there from the film of him burning the city, they must have come from his fight with The Jackal, his clothes were also burned but they were durable enough. If the Jackal did that to him, then she can take him down – but she did not wish to take him down. And she did not know he purposely got himself burned.

She stopped at a near grovel road with big and tall trees on either side that clothed everything within them in darkness. At least they did not cover the gravel road. The rain poured harder, the clouds grumbled and intermittently flashed lightning.

Amanirenas's hair made her look even more seductive in the rain, she was scowling at Pygmy. The gravel road did not seem ideal, but Pygmy waited to hear what she would say, she had to say something. The rain was barely affecting his firm, erect dreads.

She opened her arms. "We'll fight here. No flying, no teleporting, no weapons, no energy blasts. Just good old hand-to-hand combat. If you win, I will betray Stomper and help you kill him. But if I win, you have to give me all your weapons."

Pygmy jeered. "We don't need you, Molahlehi will fight and take down Stomper by himself. Hard pass." He did not care of the reason why she would want to betray Stomper. Or what caused those burns on her skin.

Amanirenas scowled at him, she mocked him, "You are so pathetically dependent on your ability to scamper instantaneously in a fight instead of taking a hit, and use multiple weapons against someone un-armed that you would refuse to make the fight fair?"

"The same weapons you want? And fair? Fair how when you're physically stronger than The Jackal, meaning you're physically stronger than me?" Pygmy laughed. Amanirenas put her hands on her hips and rolled her eyes and responded with faint irritability, "Fine! I'll adjust my strength! And to make it even sweeter, if you win I'll date you,"

Pygmy slumped his shoulders and squinted at her. "Who said I wanna date you?"

Amanirenas got into a boxer fight stance and grunted. "Screw this, bring it on." Pygmy cast away all his weapons and got into a boxer fight stance as well and let her know, "I know the best spot for a first date," this made Amanirenas half-smile.

Pygmy got her good with a jab on the nose, making her look up at the sky. She remained like this for some seconds. She slowly looked back at him and glared. She suddenly punched him on the cheek a little too swift for him to see, but he maintained his stance, then two consecutive punches on his flank. She returned to the face and threw another to the side of his face, but he recoiled and managed to slip his arm between her already-in-motion arm and her face and hit her chin with an uppercut.

Amanirenas staggered back and thrusted her knee at him, he blocked it with both hands, but the mere impact dragged him across the gravel. He noticed she was gradually deviating from the minimum strength she had agreed to remain in, she felt stronger after every strike.

She threw a front kick, but Pygmy countered by headbutting her shin and lifting himself in the air by doing so. He spun and hit the top of her head with the heel of his foot and spun again as the speed he had spun in was in kept his body in motion. This was the part where he would normally either teleport away or use his weapons for defense as he was vulnerable mid-air, and altering his body's momentum and snapping his bones in order to evade whatever Amanirenas throws at him was not ideal as he would need his limbs functioning at a hundred percent.

Amanirenas looked up at him with rage, she threw a straight punch, he blocked it with both forearms yet the impact nearly snapped his left ulnar. He collapsed to one knee, he had his right hand on his left forearm and complained, "Hey! You said you would adjust your strength, what was that?"

Three barbs had pricked and stuck to Amanirenas's knuckles.

Amanirenas shrugged indifferently at Pygmy's question and got into a stance. Pygmy got up and responded with a smirk, "Very well, don't hold back. I won't either,"

Amanirenas teased, "Oh, is that what you always say before sex?" Pygmy had never had sex before, to be fair he had his childhood taken from him and his puberty was partially neglected as his only objective was to get stronger and exert revenge against the Sentinels. He tried not to act awkward, so that Amanirenas does not tease him some more, for if she knew she would most definitely tease him about it.

He began growing two more forearms, the extra pair of forearms did not have the vambraces, just the barbed wire all the way around to each finger. He raised his arms, perusing them, they were almost bony, there were very thin, very malnourished, and translucent.

They acted differently, all four of them, they were not subjected to the same pair's movements, this pleased him. He moved them toward each other, they went through his first visible pair, but he did feel them, he could make them interact with objects at his command. The aching bone would heal soon. This was his first technique.

He suddenly lunged at her, restrained her with the extra pair of forearms and punched her in the stomach. She grunted. She tried to headbutt him but she got the chest of his breastplate and caused a dent on it, she then began rapidly twirling at him like a drill.

His grasp slipped and her twirling at his breastplate left a whirlpool impression on his breastplate. She threw a right hook, he deflected it with the hollow forearms, before he could attack, she kicked his foot to the side and he lost balance. She quickly went over him and shoved her elbow down his spine, but he blocked it at the last moment with the forearms — they were contorted backwards. If they were his actual arms, he would have dislocated some joints.

Amanirenas was frighteningly strong, so she pushed and at the moment of impact the lightning in the distance reflected off the shiny surface of an abnormally large blade and blood splattered as it sliced her and nearly cut down deep to her veins, her reflexes saved her. The hollow forearms' barbed wire did bleed her, but they were tiny punctures.

She retreated and waited in the sky. Her forearms had thin strokes with blood dripping down as it got washed by the rain. Pygmy stood facing away from her, his hollow forearms had a 7-foot hollow sword without a handle or a guard in their hands. He turned his head with sudden jerky cracks, his head nearly turned 360 degrees.

He had a sinister grin, his eyes were empty of life, he whispered with a hiss, "If you try that again, I will end you!"

Amanirenas laughed like a mad woman, there were spherical vibrations around her clenched fists, they repelled the raindrops. She replied, "Try it!"

Pygmy spread his extra forearms as they formed as full separate pair of hollow arms, along with multiplying the sword into two, increasing their width and making the swords vantablack. This was his second technique, which he called 'The Vantablack'. He had four techniques.

"I want in on the fun!" Stomper's excited voice declared. Pygmy looked up at him, his grin quickly turned into a frown. "Gosh, you're so hard to look at. My blurry eye cries tears of joy that it can barely see. Your face is the source of all trauma-" Pygmy commented, but Stomper talked over him, he asked Amanirenas, "Why is he still alive?"

Amanirenas responded, "I was having fun with him, once he's dead, who else am I going to fight like this?"

Stomper laughed, his maniacal laughter was more menacing than Pygmy's, it was dreadful to hear, he told Amanirenas, "You can play with him as much as you want in the afterlife after I crush the both of you. Someone tried to kill me from one of our cities, they managed to kill everyone, though, with an explosion that covered the entire city and blew the curtain wall to bits. I was told you had died. So, I guess Athanasy wasn't the only traitor among us," Amanirenas paused, she did not understand why Stomper was threatening her when their common enemy stood between them. She understood how Athanasy felt. She was too stunned to speak, that, and deeply terrified — Stomper looked dead serious, that was the same face he made when he first suggested they feed him a couple of humans every time he requested — he *was* dead serious.

She was trying to discreetly seek help from Pygmy, like in those social situations where the abused tries to find subtle ways to seek help.

Pygmy stood up to Stomper. "First of all, You're not going to crush her, not until I have my date with her. Secondly, I want to see how much damage I can cause you before you kill me. Lastly, Jesus Christ, kids must gouge their eyes when you walk by. Oh, oh, can I ask; do they censor your face on TV? Or do they have like a separate R-rated program where they just exhibit that hideous mess? Odd City would have loved y-"

The entire space in that area bent and crumpled up, Stomper was vexed by Pygmy's rambling and impudence. The attack was also meant for Amanirenas, which, despite her knowing very well that Stomper was determined to kill her and that she was determined to betray him, she was starting to want another out. Neither of them were in the vicinity anymore.

Amanirenas was dragging Pygmy through the city to escape Stomper, Pygmy was flailing, yelling at her to let him go. Eventually, she did, she stopped under a bridge. The earnesty birthed by the tremendous fear was real. "We cannot fight Stomper, we need to find Molahlehi. You said he is the only one who can beat Stomper, right? Where is he?"

Pygmy reverted from his second technique and shrugged. He was so nonchalant. "He's probably toying with one of you Sentinels, that steroid puppy you mentioned. If he's not dead by now."

Amanirenas handed him his weapons, she had nabbed them before she bolted from Stomper. He thanked her jovially and cheered on to go fight Stomper, she stopped him and yelled at him, "Didn't you hear me? What is wrong with you? You can never, ever hope to even scathe Stomper with a fraction of The Jackal's power when the rest of the Sentinels have full power but cannot fight him!"

Pygmy replied as he stretched, "I'm going to fight him. If I run away I'll just have nightmares of his haunting face. I already have enough trauma."

"You really don't care if you die, do you?"

"No, I'm tired. While you and your Sentinels were having orgies and partying and indulging in your luxuries with those things you call humans, we were suffering in the darkness day in and out for years losing our sanities and what made us human. We lived off of pure hate for all of you, and even now I am battling against myself not to disembowel you with my third technique and bathe in your blood.

"I like you, I haven't liked anyone like this since... Pepa. And yes, I don't even know you personally apart from the Sentinels of Anathema's title, but I do like you this quick, because I'm desperately starved of emotions. So, I cling onto the faintest bit of romance, and I cannot stand liking you because I want to kill you — so I rather die, I'm not emotionally equipped nor prepared to handle liking someone. My mind is already in shambles. We are all destined to die, it happens faster in wars, I'm no exception."

Amanirenas sighed and replied, "Well, you didn't win back there, but I did break the rules a couple of times. So, let's make a bet; you're going to die first against Stomper,"

Pygmy snorted. "I don't doubt that."

He teleported away, Amanirenas growled and launched to the sky. The race to see who would die first had begun.

CHAPTER 19
EYES TO SEE, LIPS TO SMILE

Pygmy appeared before Stomper on the rooftop, who had been expecting him and had predicted his apparition. He told Pygmy, "Ever since you and your friends crawled out from wherever you came from, life for us, Sentinels, and our human herd has been misery. You being here I can only assume you have killed The Jackal. I have a burning desire to kill you and all of your friends." The feeling was mutual from Pygmy and his friends' side.

Pygmy was holding his short swords, he shrugged as he snickered, this agitated Stomper. He caused the space around Pygmy's flanks to crumple, but Pygmy teleported away and appeared on the edge of the rooftop. His breastplate was crumpled on the sides and fell off him, Stomper almost got him. He laughed, "Such a cowardly power you possess. It merely helps you run away faster."

"Molahlehi told me your parents had the same power." Pygmy replied monotonously.

This fazed Stomper, but its effect was ephemeral. Stomper, when he was still young, was physically abused by his father on a regular basis, sometimes it was less severe, when he came home drunk it was most severe. Stomper's mother had run away with another man to get away from Stomper's father as she had also become a victim to his abuse, leaving poor little Stomper alone with his abusive father. His father blamed him for his mother leaving them, and unbridled his abuse upon Stomper.

One of Stomper's teachers had noticed the ever-growing contusions on Stomper's body and had called the cops, that was the last time Stomper saw his father — he ran away from the cops and was never seen again. There were rumors that he had fled the country, but that didn't matter, Stomper was free. It seemed like a low blow for Pygmy, but to be fair Stomper and the other Sentinels were responsible for what Pygmy had become, for his parents' deaths.

Stomper clenched his fists, Pygmy had succeeded in goading him, Pygmy jumped off the edge of the rooftop while giving Stomper the finger. The entire building disassembled in a single explosive force, as if being pulled to different directions by an invisible force, this was Stomper's doing, Pygmy felt pressure around his body, this pressure paralyzed him, he attempted to teleport away, but this inexplicably rising pressure impeded him from doing so.

Stomper suddenly appeared before him, and hammered his massive fist down Pygmy, the force of impact rippled across Pygmy's body and shook his brain, it felt like he had died for a moment, he catapulted to the ground, causing an aperture through the tar road and continued down a few dozen feet underground. Everything turned black, his heart stopped beating, but he was still alive.

The building's debris rained everywhere along with Pygmy's scattered weapons. It was a surprise that his clothes did not tear away. Perhaps if he had his breastplate Stomper's fist would not have been felt so severely. Stomper stood above the hole, his thirst for more was brimming. He uttered his hand, his palm open, and blocked the transparent laser beam of energy from Amanirenas, the beam had no effect on Stomper. She shifted the target to his face, he did not block, just to spite her. It hit his face and well, it did nothing to him. Until the laser thinned, he ducked as he felt its sudden effect, it grazed his head. This made him angry.

He bombarded Amanirenas with his space-bending explosions, she scurried away. Pygmy appeared suddenly before him, his eyes were dark gray and empty, he didn't seem conscious. Stomper focused his space-benders to hem him in and prevent him from teleporting away. But Pygmy had not intention to run away, he looked hollow, like a phantom. Then, his third technique activated. Dozens of hollow vantablack swords appeared spinning haphazardly around Pygmy's midriff, they cut through Stomper's energy and gifted Stomper with numerous superficial cuts as he recoiled and retreated from the area. The blades cut through anything and everything, they spun out of control, slicing the buildings and vehicles around him and they even damaged the ground. Then, they suddenly stopped and vanished as quick as they had appeared, and Pygmy came to, he was breathing laboriously. He hopped away as the ground caved in.

He stood on a balcony, gazing at Stomper with not a trace of his usual frivolity. His facial expression was neutral. Amanirenas came back, she scanned the area and asked Pygmy what had happened. He replied in a low, flat tone, "My third technique, it uses the vantablack swords, but there's a downside to it,"

"It would appear I may have struck a nerve, or punched some sense into you. No more jokes, huh?" Stomper laughed spitefully.

The black, hollow arms protruded from Pygmy's back carrying two 12-foot vantablack swords, he carried one and the let one hollow hand carry the other. Amanirenas noticed a change in his aura, he was not spewing nonsense or making jokes. It gave her a tingling sensation. She stretched and popped her knuckles. "Okay then, I guess we're going to try to kill him instead of racing to see who would die first. Then, I'll go all out."

Pygmy knew Stomper's abilities were the space-benders, which could either crumple or explode, but he did not know they could bend the space around him to render his teleportation ability inactive. But those space-benders were not Stomper's only abilities.

A sudden seismic activity worried both Pygmy and Amanirenas, the vibrations even altered the shapes of the raindrops and vigorously shook them right where they were. The ground was not the only thing trembling, even the sky was trembling. Amanirenas and Pygmy looked at each other with apprehension. A disembodied woman's sudden shriek from the sky and beneath the ground blew away the buildings, their foundations, and the tar to every direction — scraping the ground.

Amanirenas and Pygmy nimbly avoided the chaotically shifting infrastructure. Everything was shoved to the surrounding area. When it stopped, all the city's infrastructure was disorderly piled up in a 180 feet radius around them. It had formed a poor emulation of a gladiators arena. Amanirenas had no idea Stomper could perform such harrowing feats, Pygmy was equally disturbed of Stomper's godly power. Stomper opened his arms and said a menacing tone, "I did this all for you two. So, please do not disappoint me." But all they could see was his silhouette in the moted arena as the rain fought to flatten the dust in the air.

The dust began to settle quickly. It was time.

Amanirenas was able to sense for an unreliably short amount of time when Stomper's energy accumulated before he blows or crumples or weaponizes space, but it was not very helpful because she could not keep up half the time. She was hoping she finds a way to keep up, or she would be the first to lose the dance of death.

Pygmy appeared suddenly before Stomper, invading his personal space, Stomper punched him on the right cheek, the force of impact rippled through Pygmy's skull, Amanirenas rushed in to help. Pygmy used the excess force of Stomper's punch to twirl his body even faster and kick Stomper's tooth with the heel of his foot, shattering it away. Amanirenas sensed Stomper's coercion bulk up around Pygmy's body, it impeded Pygmy from teleporting.

She slipped in between them and punched Stomper in the chest, he growled and used his explosive force, but she retreated her arm from those minuscule explosions, but they managed to tear the surface of her skin, leaving a patch of red.

She screamed in ire as laser-focused energy beams shot out of her eyes. Stomper stretched his mouth wide open and absorbed all of it — in fact he did more than just absorb the incoming beams, he was sucking them out of Amanirenas's eyes, Amanirenas noticed this and attempted to cease, but Stomper was not letting go of her energy, he continued to tug it. She panicked and shut her eyes, which worked, which also was part of Stomper's intentions. He reached out to grab her fast with malicious intent.

Pygmy pulled her out of the way with his left hand as he simultaneously with his right hollow hand struck down Stomper's hand in hopes of snithing it. But the vantablack sword slipped from his grasp and hurled far into the pile of infrastructure around them before making contact, it felt like something or someone had plucked it from his hand.

He felt a rise in the oppressive force around his body that hindered him from teleporting, this meant Stomper would attack. And he did. Pygmy could not use his third technique as Amanirenas would get caught in the crossfire, the third technique seemed like an ideal solution to ending Stomper — if done right. So he stuck to his second technique. A gigantic vantablack sword appeared in the sky and smote Stomper as Pygmy and Amanirenas retreated. Mud splattered everywhere and the ground lurched.

Right. Mud. The ground was getting muddy, the rain was pouring endlessly. Amanirenas slowly opened her eyes, she felt a sting that made her eyes watery. Her vision was temporarily blurred, but she did not tell Pygmy because it quickly got back to normal, and she was determined not to be the first to go out.

She inquired, "What was that sound? What happened? Is that...?"

Pygmy responded, his eyes fixed forward, "Yes, another vantablack sword. I can do that. I wanted to use my third technique, but you would have been collateral damage."

"I thought you burned with a desire to kill us Sentinels," Amanirenas teased him. He responded in a flat tone, "There's no guarantee that my third technique *can* kill Stomper, the only deducible thing is that he would rather avoid it than block it, and it can in fact harm him. But 'harm' and 'kill' are two different things." He was honestly impressed with Amanirenas's physical strength, but he was not about to say it.

Pygmy perceived clearly, Stomper had blocked his gigantic vantablack sword, but what pleased Pygmy was the blood dripping down Stomper's palms. He almost smiled. Amanirenas began shooting her energy blasts at Stomper, targeting his little finger. Stomper growled, the more blows his finger took, the more Pygmy felt his sword cutting deeper into his palm.

Pygmy maintained the pressure of the sword down Stomper, and beckoned with his index finger, the vantablack sword he'd lost catapulted from the beyond the stage straight toward Stomper. When Amanirenas blew Stomper's finger to bits, there was another disembodied shriek, it was piercing.

It blew away the rain drops, scattered the clouds, fragmented Pygmy's gigantic vantablack sword, and blew the catapulting sword back into the piled-up infrastructure. Pygmy shoved the vantablack sword he was holding deep into the ground with his hollow hands to keep himself from being blown away while shutting his ears with the original pair. He saw, for the first time, ripples on a muddy ground.

Amanirenas also had her ears shut from the piercing shriek, but she was strong enough to stand as she was without the explosive force pushing her or blowing her away. This went on for half a minute.

Stomper was suddenly in front of Pygmy, his speed was mimicking Pygmy's teleportation. He stuck his thumbs into the corners of Pygmy's lips and tore Pygmy's skin as he ran his thumbs angularly to portray a smile across his cheeks, he laughed, "There's that smile! " blood gushed from Pygmy's ragged cheeks. Stomper used his space-benders to blow him away as he swung his iklwa at him, he was not even close to scratching Stomper. Then, on to the next. He targeted Amanirenas, he lunged to her so fast it looked he had teleported.

He had his mouth gaping in case she uses her laser beams — the darkness in his mouth was terrifying. Amanirenas made the skulking energies before her eyes and maneuvered to escape them, the explosions nearly claimed her eyes. Stomper clenched his massive fist threw a punch at her, she reciprocated. Their fists collided, the collision made Amanirenas jolt and compelled her to firmly plant her foot onto the ground so she is not overpowered.

Stomper never liked Amanirenas's might, it made his skin crawl, and seeing her able to stop his punch stoked his anger. He promptly unclenched his fist and covered Amanirenas's fist with his gigantic hand. Amanirenas was aghast when she figured out what he was trying to do — he was trying to squash her hand.

She summoned as much energy as she could to shroud her fist as she frantically tried to escape. Stomper yanked her around as he vibrated with laughter. Then, abruptly, her eyes popped and fluids squirted past her eyelids, the explosions, this distracted her as she was briefly stuck in a stupor, this loosened the concentrated energy shrouding her hand. Stomper crushed her hand and blew her away with his space-benders, leaving only her hand crushed inside his.

CHAPTER 20
HE'S DEAD, HE'S ALIVE, HE'S HOLLOW

Amanirenas was sobbing, she had lost her eyes and her right hand — her dominant hand. She sat in the mud using her concentrated energy to plug the gash that flooded out blood that her hand being torn from her arm left. The rain returned and was making it difficult for her hearing. She wanted to crawl to Pygmy to heal him as well, she had seen Stomper rip his skin apart in a malicious attempt to force him to smile, she worried about him.

Pygmy was lying on the mud, facing up at the rain as he gurgled and choked in his own blood, the rain was making it impossible for the wounds to close up, so blood did not stop pouring out. He was still conscious, still alive, watching the clouded sky weep. He laid sprawled, lost in empty thoughts.

'People like you start wars to murder whoever to win and come out on top, people like me, well, we keep the war going for as long as possible without a care of who wins or loses, as long as there are still people breathing, we won't stop - and that's why people like me don't like to start fights, but people like you like to start fights. I burned the code to the gate wall, so no one will escape. You see, I'm not like

you, I'm worse than you.' He had learned those words from Molahlehi.

He heard Amanirenas call for him, her voice was trembling, he jerked up and coughed out the rainwater that had puddled in his mouth and had become mottled with his blood. He turned over and applied pressure on the bleeding with his hollow hands while he used his solid hands to sit up. He felt his heart jolt painfully when he saw Amanirenas crawling on the mud glauming and calling his name, he teleported to her.

She felt him, she quickly grasped for his face with the only hand she had left, and told him, "Please, remove your hands. I can stop the bleeding using the pressure of my energy. It's okay,"

Pygmy slowly removed his hands with hesitation, he was deeply concerned for her, he wanted to say something about her eyes, her hand as well, but he could not speak. Stomper was not as dull as one might have presumed, he ensured that Amanirenas, without her sight, and Pygmy, without his words, would not guide each other in the battle. Pygmy would not be able to warn her about Stomper's movements, and Amanirenas would not be able to spot Stomper's space-benders and warn Pygmy should they be aimed at him.

She asked Pygmy to close his mouth so she could reattach his skin, but he stopped her with his hands and shook his head, she asked hesitantly, "You don't want me to reattach it?" he nodded. She wanted to ask why, but Pygmy was a deeply disturbed, damaged and peculiar one. So, she merely closed the bleeding wounds without attaching his cheeks back together — leaving his teeth exposed — of course the edges of his cheeks were reattached so his jaw does not fall out. He was up to something.

He was frightening to look at, but he had nothing on Stomper. He gently grabbed her wrist and drew his finger in the center, she was confounded, she asked, unsure of what he was trying to say, "You... want to have sex?" she placed her hand on the side of his face to read his gestures, he shook his head. But, he did, if they survive, but that was not what he was trying to tell her.

He summoned his short vantablack spear, she realized what he was suggesting, she prepared herself by taking a deep breath, and nodded to signal him that she was ready. He stuck his index and middle finger inside the center, opening the wound, but Amanirenas did not cry — pain was not outlandish to her.

She had cried when Stomper popped her eyes solely because they were advantageous in this battle. Blood ran down as the rain washed it away from the open wound, Pygmy slowly stuck the spear inside, he was inserting it slowly so she can tell him if it is too deep. She asked him to stop at a specific point, then, she used her only hand to close up the wound socket around the spear. She thanked him.

They both turned to Stomper's hands applauding mirthfully, he laughed and shouted, "Don't tell me you're done, already. I am still warming up."

Amanirenas put her hand on the side of Pygmy's face, she felt his snag teeth, she whispered as she slowly swiveled her head, "Nod when I'm facing directly at him,"

Pygmy nodded when she faced him and she put her hand down. He did not know what she was planning, but he was dubious of its success. The only person who could kill Stomper was Molahlehi, but where was he? He should have arrived at the last moment before Stomper maimed them.

Amanirenas was baring her teeth at Stomper, she was furious. In a blink of an eye, Pygmy's eyes widened to the droplets that halted around Amanirenas, she blasted from the spot straight to Stomper. A sudden strong wave blasted the raindrops to every direction. It nearly blew Pygmy away.

She snatched Stomper and dragged him across the arena, past the infrastructure, and throughout the rest of the city building to building. She had stabbed him on the left man boob with the vantablack spear and had her left fist pressed against his right boob enveloped by her pressurized energy, she fortunately managed to break two of his ribs. Stomper tried to grab her arms, but it was strenuous to do so as she was moving at very rapid speed, in fact, they ended up exiting the city into the wilderness. Stomper managed to move his arms and attempted crushing both her arms, but she had numerous layers of her energy shrouding her entire body. He punched her on the side of the face, but the layers were too thick.

At the arena, Pygmy got up and started stretching. He bounced off the balls of his heels, took a deep breath, then activated his fourth and last technique.

The pair hollow hands and forearms detached and turned into the pair of hollow hands and arms, now he had four arms again. But it did not stop there. A third pair of arms jutted from his shoulders, this pair was skeletal with barbs, it was not hollow, it was solid and pale. This skeletal pair had its own pair of protruded shoulder blades. From his calves jutted out a pair of barbed skeletal hocks that stood steadfast on the mud.

The barbed skeletal pair carried the vantablack swords, while the hollow hands carried vantablack versions of the short swords, and in his solid fleshly hands he carried vantablack versions of the Zulu axe and the iklwa.

The final touches to the fourth technique became visible on his face, his face split into two conjoined faces. He had three eyes, the other face was skeletal — a barbed skull, and the other his regular darkened face. The eye in the middle that the two faces shared was hollow and empty. Before he teleported away, he brought one of the enormous vantablack weapons hovering in the air to his side.

Stomper began crushing the layers around Amanirenas's arms, there were cracks as though bones breaking. They hit a curtain wall and blasted through the buildings, then hit a second curtain wall as they exited. They had passed through one of the cities, but there were no living citizens in the city, it was empty. There were piles of dead bodies and a fleeting odor as they swiftly passed by. Someone had massacred the entire city, it was Shirley.

In a second past the wilderness into the other city, when they hit the curtain wall, Amanirenas promptly withdrew her arms from the layers and shoved the spear, aiming for Stomper's eye, but due to her being blind, she instead shoved it into his left nostril.

Stomper crushed the layers she had left behind and used his space-benders to blow up her midriff, but she had kept a few layers around herself, so the explosion staved the layers and she was projected to the sky as Stomper came to a stop in the middle of this city.

His back was frayed and bled, this upset him. He pulled out the spear from his nostril and crushed it in his hand, it broke like glass. There was that odor again, he looked around and saw a horrific sight of the entire populace of the city slaughtered. He gasped at the sight.

He dived forward to evade the large vantablack sword that nearly smote him, he turned while in the air and crumpled the sword, then another vantablack sword swung diagonally at him, he merely glanced at it and it fragmented into a million pieces and it blew right past him. When he landed, he felt something being crushed under his foot, he raised his foot and what he saw made his wrath take control of him, it was corpse of a human, he had accidentally stepped on its skull.

Before his wrath could get the best of him, he hopped away to escape the blades of both vantablack swords, this time they were swung by Pygmy, he was standing in front of him. He felt Stomper's energy hem in on his body, Stomper clenched his fist and threw it at Pygmy, but Pygmy managed to teleport away, and all that was left constricted by Stomper's pressure was the hollow him — a frozen shadow figure, holding the short swords. Stomper was baffled, his fist went right through the shadow.

Pygmy abruptly appeared above the shadow figure's head hammering down his axe at Stomper's head, Stomper tipped his head to the side and Pygmy grazed his ear and lodged the axe into Stomper's clavicle.

Stomper had him, instead of constraining him, he was going to kill him by using his explosive space-benders to inflate his throat, but the shards blasting everywhere shocked Stomper, Amanirenas had shrouded him with her energy. But how? She was blind. Stomper figured it out immediately, it was from when she touched his face after she whispered something to him – it had to be.

Stomper sent an explosion, Pygmy teleported away and appeared on top two vehicles that had been consumed by fire. Stomper crumpled the vantablack version of the axe and cast it to the side. Before he could ask Pygmy if he was responsible for the slaughter of his people, the iklwa fell from the sky and stabbed his head, but unfortunately its speed was not enough to get it to sink deep into Stomper's thick skin. Stomper had winced when it stabbed his head but then he was greatly annoyed, he fragmented it away and the shadow figure before him.

Pygmy was now left with four arms. The hollow him was gone. Stomper yelled at him with rageful vehemence in his voice, "How could you? How many of my people did you slaughter?" He demanded answers.

Pygmy snickered, ah, he was back. He counted with his fingers and the skeletal fingers and mouthed sentences Stomper did not understand. Pygmy then pointed at his mouth. Of course, he could not talk anymore, he would murmur if her tried to speak. But something occurred to Stomper, how could he not talk?

Pygmy yelled, "Now!" The ground beneath Stomper's feet blew as Amanirenas's energy exploded and sent him aloft. Pygmy soared after Stomper. Amanirenas emerged underground. Pygmy suddenly appeared before Stomper's face in the clear sky, he ran his vantablack sword across Stomper's forearm as Stomper blocked it, bits of blood splashed. Stomper used his explosive space-benders, but Pygmy had suddenly disappeared. There was another cut on Stomper's right shoulder, but he did not see Pygmy.

Was it possible that he was invisible? As Stomper wondered there was another cut across his leg, when he glanced down he did not see Pygmy anywhere, but he had felt his ephemeral presence. Then, another cut across his face. It started making sense to Stomper now, Pygmy did appear, but he was exceptionally quick that he was just impossible to spot.

Stomper surrounded himself with those bits of constraining coercions that impeded Pygmy from teleporting, Pygmy was not Amanirenas, so he did not see the trap Stomper had set for him.

Another cut that ran through both Stomper's calves, Stomper grunted and turned with a scowl to see. It had worked! He got him! Pygmy was stuck in the air, he had vantablack versions of his daggers in his hands, but the barbed skeleton was detached from him. Stomper decided it was futile if it appears again, he could easily ensnare it as he did Pygmy. As he thought this, it appeared, the vantablack swords from above and from below lodged into his forearm in a failed attempt to cut off his arm. Stomper was stunned to see Amanirenas had also teleported — but Amanirenas could not teleport. She was toting the sword that struck him from below, and the barbed skeleton was... The skeleton had managed to escape.

Stomper had an outburst and crimpled everything around him, including Amanirenas and Pygmy, but they were suddenly gone had narrowly slipped from his snare. He knew what had happened, the barbed skeleton had appeared and teleported them away. It made sense, Amanirenas could not teleport, it was the barbed skeleton's doing. Stomper had to crush it. It was their only advantage against him.

CHAPTER 21
EPITHET OF FIRE

Amanirenas and Pygmy appeared on top of the curtain wall to Stomper's side. Pygmy and the barbed skeleton were once again one. Stomper fragmented away the vantablack swords. Now the only vantablack weapons — which were the only type of weapons in Pygmy's arsenal that could harm Stomper — were the daggers. He could not make more as they exhausted him. The daggers could only cut the surface of Stomper's skin, they could not dig into the flesh like the vantablack swords. It seemed the result of this battle remained the same — Stomper could not be beaten.

Stomper knew that his victory was inexorable, these two could never hope to take him down. Especially when he had his own other techniques he was yet to display, but it seemed he would not need to resort to them. He was winning with merely his space-benders and the fragmentation technique. His large-scale repulsive woman's shriek was another technique. His injuries slowly started healing themselves, his frayed back's skin spread threads like a spider's web as it reattached itself.

He wiped his nose as the inside of his nostrils healed the gash caused by Amanirenas shoving the spear into his nose. So, it would not have mattered if Amanirenas had slashed his eye. Pygmy notified Amanirenas of what was happening. She sighed and responded hopelessly, "I didn't know he could do that." Pygmy also had no knowledge of this special clandestine ability of Stomper's because nothing had ever harmed Stomper so he could reveal his healing ability.

Pygmy did not attempt to uplift Amanirenas, he told her, "You told me before we started fighting him that the Sentinels as a whole could never hope to take him down. And I never believed we would win." now he sounded disheartened. "I was just stalling him, in hopes that Molahlehi shows up."

Amanirenas clicked her tongue. "Where *is* Molahlehi?" Pygmy shrugged, forgetting she could not see anymore. He held her left hand with the barbed skeleton hand, and said, he sounded less disheartened, "If Molahlehi isn't coming, then we won't continue fighting. It is impossible to beat Stomper. I know a place..."

"A place for...?" Amanirenas asked, then she quickly understood. A place for their first date. Stomper turned to face them, he was good as new, Pygmy said to Amanirenas, not minding Stomper, "It's a full moon tonight, so it'll be great when the sun sets," it was dusk. It would soon be nightfall. Stomper inferred they were planning on attacking him, so he steadied himself to unleash one of his other techniques, Pygmy would not let the chance pass to give him the finger before they teleport away.

Pygmy looked at her and told her, "You lost two bets today. You were definitely going to die first in that battle."

Amanirenas sighed, he was right, she admitted it, but commented sarcastically, "Nevermind me being blinded forever and losing my hand. You won the bet, that's all that matters." He shrugged, guess he was that kind of person.

Before they could instantaneously flee, and before Stomper could attack, a gale blew, accompanied by scents and unease that claimed their attention. The wind came from the direction of Pygmy, Molahlehi and Shirley's hiding place. The multiple scents made Stomper ravenous, they frightened Pygmy, and they bewildered Amanirenas.

Pygmy teleported to that area, unsuspectingly evading Stomper's surprise attack. Thanks to Amanirenas dragging Stomper over a vast distance earlier, he was even farther away from the hideout. He flew as fast as he could toward the area of the strange activity.

Pygmy appeared before a silver, circular, big metal trapdoor in the tall grass. On the other side of it, in the sky, was Molahlehi. He was staring at the sky. Pygmy reverted from his fourth technique and yelled, it felt out of character to yell at Molahlehi, it made his stomach turn, but he was angry and confused, so he yelled,

"Teacher, what did you do? What are you doing? I needed you back there, *we* needed you!"

Molahlehi looked down at him and Amanirenas, he was indifferent to what could only be a team-up with a Sentinel of Anathema. Oh, Anathema. Pygmy yelled again, "Why did you release them? Stomper is still alive and he's coming here. Our mission is not complete yet."

Amanirenas smelled what Molahlehi had released, it was a smell she had not smelled in so long that it felt outlandish. She began thinking about it, about this supposed mission Pygmy mentioned. Molahlehi, Shirley, and Pygmy had hundreds of humans, actual, pure humans not those extensions of Anathema, deep underground. They were planning on releasing them after they burned down all the Sentinels' cities and eradicated the Sentinels. They wanted to restore the old world. But why was Molahlehi releasing them now?

"Do you remember that episode of Odd City where those archeologists unearthed a statue of a horned bestial creature with wings?" Molahlehi asked, no expression in his voice. Pygmy waited to hear what he would say, he continued, "For years, people thought it was a demon, but that anonymous occultist they interviewed explained its true meaning. But people did not care, and in their united belief of its nature, they converted its nature to a demonic one. It's the same with the Epithet of Fire, or, as you were led to believe..."

Amanirenas sensed an oppressive, familiar presence crawling into this reality, she took a step back in horror and whispered as her lips shuddered, "Anathema."

The sky shook as all sounds went mute, the grass stopped wavering and came to a standstill. Pygmy looked at Amanirenas, then back at Molahlehi, he was fearful of what this might have meant. It made sense why Molahlehi woke up and released those humans. He was summoning Anathema, and would offer them as a sacrifice. But why? They did not need Anathema. They were executing the Sentinels of Anathema for this sole purpose — they had used millions of humans as sacrifices in exchange for their powers.

Pygmy blinked, and in his one good eye, before his lid shut, he captured a figure in the sky that wasn't there half a second ago. Why was he blinking, how could he blink? Of course, the downside of using his third technique was overpowering fatigue. He staggered, he felt dizzy, then, he gathered himself and looked up again. There it was.

"Pygmy, I don't know what's happening or why Anathema is being summoned, but we need to get as far away from here as possible. Anathema is unpredictable, he is evil incarnate. He-" Amanirenas was speaking when she felt Anathema probing inside her, inside her powers, but they were his powers, and he lived inside them as he did every human being in those 35 cities.

That was the reason why Pygmy longed for death for so long but could not kill himself. Why Bullpit stood up to Stomper knowing he would die if he ever fought him. Why Yoddha did not retreat for help when Shirley revealed what her nanobots were doing to his body. Why Athanasy left with Stomper and The Jackal knowing Stomper would try to kill her and another reason why she provoked him to kill her in that blob.

Amanirenas felt his malicious intent, he was about to do something to her, but not just her, Pygmy, too, Stomper as well. Stomper plummeted from the sky as Anathema awoke inside him, then, altogether with Molahlehi and the fifty humans and Anathema, they were teleported to the arena. Stomper crashed into the muddy ground, it was still cloudy in that area, but the rain was waning.

Anathema was a colossal being, his entire body from his head to his feet was of a stellar view, his skin had stars, planets, quasars, meteors, black holes, galaxies, etc. His eyes were of a moon and a sun, his right eye was a sun, and the left a moon. His afro was widespread and was made of a blue sky with clouds, it was said to be a good omen when the sky was clear, and bad luck when his sky was cloudy and gloomy, but those were nothing more than theories — he was unbridledly evil.

His very presence never indicated anything auspicious. He was draped in a big cloak with lenticular prints, from one side it appeared as a close-up view of an agitated ocean, another view of a lava, and the other of running mud.

Majestic above them, his presence was felt at every corner of the arena. The aimlessly wandering humans were teleported sparsely into the broken city. Pygmy, Amanirenas, and Stomper felt Anathema's grip loosening around their souls as he slowly slithered away and disappeared. They knew he was responsible for bringing them into the arena, but Molahlehi was not shocked, if anything he knew of Anathema's agenda — but of course he would know, he conjured him into the corporeal realm.

Amanirenas was panicking, she pleaded with Pygmy to tell her what has happening and who had conjured Anathema, he gnashed at Molahlehi. Molahlehi gave Pygmy a cold, empty look, but if you stared long enough, you would start to see some pity. He stared at Anathema, and began, "Do you know why I mentioned that episode? Because, this is the same as it. Let me tell you a story to explain my actions — not justify them."

"Odd City was debunked, there's nothing altruistic about that demon." Pygmy yelled at Molahlehi, who was indifferent to his rage.

Stomper recognized Molahlehi, but was baffled to see that he was capable of summoning Anathema, as far as he knew, the Sentinels were the first and only ones to discover Anathema's existence, and Athanasy was the only one who could summon him. Molahlehi started, "Three centuries ago, there lived a small, wise, powerful tribe called the Gondras. The Gondras could, after generations of consistent dedication to fire, conjure and manipulate fire.

"We lived reclusively, hidden from the outside world. Our tribe was too prudent to be tempted by the power we had over fire. Nothing could ever go wrong in such a society except the temptation of one to be dominant over all fire. Or so we thought.

"Our united power manifested our egregore. The chief called this majestic being the Epithet of Fire, *our* Epithet of Fire. This being you all now know of as Anathema," he scowled at Stomper, then relaxed his face, he continued, "It lingered in our sky for days, days turned to weeks, then months. We had no desire to communicate with it, as it was our egregore, so there was no need to.

"One day, it spoke to us, it told us it served us, and would grant us any wish imaginable. We were advised by the chief to tread carefully, he allowed us to make the wishes. Each wish free. We could control fire, we could heal ourselves, we were one with nature, we didn't need anything. Except, we were not immune to death.

"Most wished for the return of their loved ones who had died long ago, the Epithet of Fire granted them their wishes without demanding anything in return. This worried the tribe. The chief found out the price to its wishes, he told them the Epithet of Fire demanded their fire in exchange, sucking the fire out of their life force — they were deviating from their righteous paths. It was hard to believe, but our desires for wishes poisoned our egregore, and it poisoned us. The entire tribe heeded this warning, they noticed later their fire slowly dying, they then abandoned their egregore. But, it did not go away. Our fire could not hurt it, no matter how hard we tried. We did not know egregores could be separated from the group. It still loomed in our sky.

"One day, the chief wished for it to go away, it worked, but at the cost of ten men and women's lives, then, it lived within them. We had since then detached ourselves from it. It went on to grant wishes and take more and more lives, the cost of a single wish was progressively becoming too much to pay. So, we abandoned our way of fire and unified society, scattering around the country, hoping it would work. And it did, the Epithet of Fire disappeared from the earth, but it was by that time known as Anathema."

"Are you the chief?" Pygmy bluntly asked. Molahlehi nodded slowly. Stomper walked toward them and discarded, "Impossible! You did not achieve immortality. How have you lived for so many years?" He sought the elixir of life himself, he would slaughter them after hearing how Molahlehi achieved it... Or, there were fifty humans running around in the city. He had a bad idea.

He turned to Anathema to make his wish; "Anathema, make me immor—" he choked. So did Pygmy and Amanirenas. They fell to the muddy ground almost simultaneously. Molahlehi told him, "You are too late. I wished for the Epithet of Fire to banish itself from the corporeal realm and take every part of it with it, in exchange of... human lives." He sounded ashamed.

Pygmy was too busy having a seizure to react, but he then felt nothing but hatred for his former teacher. All their hard work, done away by a single wish — a wish of a traitor.

Molahlehi said to Pygmy as everything got dark and the three of them passed out, "I am truly sorry, Pygmy. I had to rectify my tribe's mistake. There's a lot you're too young to understand. Including parts of the story. By the time you wake up, all of Anathema's might will have ceased, the three of you will be free from him, human again. You can choose to kill Stomper, he will be just a normal human being like you."

CHAPTER 22
POSTBELLUM

Pygmy woke up in a haste, he sought Molahlehi, it felt like he had just woken up from a very bad, long nightmare. But it was not a nightmare, it was all real, he was in the arena. It was nighttime. He felt different, a lot different. Like he was fully present in the moment aware of everything and feeling everything around him, the air he breathed did not feel so outlandish anymore.

He was back to being wholly human, devoid of Anathema, rather, the Epithet of Fire's essence and inconspicuous influence. His face was clear of the darkness, his eyes reverted from those gray circles to normal human eyes. His Nevus of Ota was now a full black circle around his eye. He felt a slight pain from his permanent wide smile, but it felt like it had healed a long time ago.

He turned over to Amanirenas when he heard her groaning, he crawled to her and woke her up. If not for the full moon, it would have been pitch black, and, with his human eyes (not forgetting the blurred one), it was relatively difficult to see in the dark. Amanirenas softly called his name, he sniffled. "Yeah, it's me,"

He helped her up, she asked him, irritated by his previous ignorance to her previous questions, "What happened? Is it... all over?"

Oh, how those words brought immense longing to Pygmy, how he wished it were all over – but there were people still breathing. Shirley had told him not to worry about her, so he did not, but he wished he could see her. It would be nice for her to be the first person he sees when this nightmare ends. But this nightmare was practically over, Pygmy just had to close this trauma-laden book and stow it as far as he could — he could only do this by killing Stomper. It did not bother him that Amanirenas was still breathing, he preferred keeping her, just one person from the war, breathing – then he will stop.

He turned to look into Stomper's direction, but he was gone. He was not as invincible as he used to be, he was human, flesh and blood, susceptible to death. Pygmy was brimming with excitement. Now Stomper could not hide under his over-powered techniques and abilities.

Pygmy told Amanirenas, he sounded more sane, "It's not, not yet. I have to find and kill Stomper, then you and I can go find those humans" he was back to being wholly part of *the humans* "wandering in the city. The feral beasts out there were not mutated by Anathema, so they are still creeping out there,"

"Then, our first date," Amanirenas reminded him, she was blushing. She looked as though she were unburdened, the absence of the Epithet of Fire was distinctly visible in both of them. Unfortunately, like Pygmy's injuries, she maintained her injuries in human form.

Pygmy swallowed, he was sweating, his palms felt slippery, the cold sweat trickling from his armpits made him shiver. He mustered the courage, he asked her nervously, "Can I... kiss you?"

Amanirenas could feel his elevated breath not too close to her face, but she could point out where it came from. She leaned in and kissed him on the lips. She had her hand on the side of his torn face. The kiss was odd with Pygmy's free makeover by Stomper, but it was somehow better than kissing Bullpit's dog lips. Pygmy could not make up his mind about whether to put his hands on her waist or on her face or to grab her posterior.

After the kiss, he opened his eyes and had hoped to look into Amanirenas's eyes, briefly forgetting that the vile monster Stomper had taken her sight. Amanirenas asked him, with a slight tease in her tone, "I can't tell if it's your first kiss or not, especially with what Stomper did to your face. Is it your first kiss?"

Pygmy cleared his throat, he saw a flash of light of the moon as something pierced the air, it was heading toward them, and it was too fast. Amanirenas turned, she twisted her body suddenly to try to catch this projectile with both hands, but she had forgotten that she only possessed one hand. She managed to catch it with one hand — though both reached to grab the projectile. Pygmy was also fast enough, he caught the projectile with one hand, as he could not use both hands as he did not think he merely acted.

The projectile, due to its frightening speed, albeit the efforts of Pygmy and Amanirenas's hand to halt it, managed to pierce Amanirenas's shoulder and hit a major blood vessel. The force of impact pushed her and she bumped into Pygmy. Both their palms were scorched and scraped by the projectile, fortunately it did not go through her shoulder, it only got lodged inside. It seemed their combined effort had worked, it could have been worse.

It *was* worse, Amanirenas had not felt such heightened pain in human form in a very long time, she did not scream or cry, but she did groan over and over. The projectile was a steel rod. Hurled by none other than Stomper. Pygmy was impressed of Amanirenas's quick reflexes despite her being blinded. He gnashed at the direction the steel rod came from and told her, "It's Stomper, I'm going after him."

He had to get her out of range in case he hurls another steel rod. He peered around desperately as he scurried with Amanirenas to hiding, hoping to spot something in the mud to hurl back at Stomper, but even if he could find something, it was not humanly possible to throw something at that force and speed over that vast distance.

Had Stomper maintained his super strength or was he a very strong man? This slightly worried Pygmy because he knew the answer, Molahlehi had told him about Stomper's notorious reputation even before he had the Epithet of Fire's power. Pygmy decided he had to find some weapons, as his had faded with the Epithet of Fire. On their way near the piled-up infrastructure, another steel rod whistled past them. They seemed to have been aimed at Amanirenas. This time the throw was from a different point, but same direction, he was following their movements. Good, it made it easier for Pygmy to get to him.

He helped Amanirenas rest against a skewed wall, she was panting. He knew he had to remove the steel rod or it would cause an infection, if it had not already then it would speed up the infection. He counted down from three and pulled it out, it made her scream, it sounded like the scream might have broken her vocal chords. She swore over and over. She could not feel her arm anymore, she had a feeling it would never work again. Profuse blood poured down from the wound, Pygmy quickly pressed his hand on the wound to ease the bleeding.

She began sobbing, she cried softly, "I don't think I'm making it through the night, Pygmy."

Pygmy assertively told her she was going to live. He was panicking. He tried to teleport back to their hideout in the tall grass to fetch her some of Shirley's medical supplies, but he could not teleport anymore. This angered him, the one time he truly needed his teleportation powers to save someone they were gone. He was in denial of Amanirenas's chances. If Stomper shows up, he would be forced to release his hand from the wound and Amanirenas would bleed to death.

She told him, "Thank you so much, Pygmy. You're a kind, innocent soul that just got lost. I know you hate us Sentinels, and I know you're only helping me because you have developed feelings for me, but your mission... you just have to kill Stomper—"

"Then what? I haven't heard from Shirley, and I'm trying not to think of the worst. Molahlehi betrayed and abandoned me. You're the only pillar I can hold on to. I don't want to win if it means I'll lose everyone I care for." He responded, his voice was stable and low, his eyes clear, but Amanirenas knew he wanted to cry.

She asked him, "Before you got wrapped up in this mess. What were your aspirations?"

He looked into her eyelids, as though she were looking back. "I wanted to be a cop, like in Odd City. I wanted to fight monsters and protect people, but not like this..."

She smiled, almost empathetically. "You must know, then, if you were studying us..."

He nodded, she could not see his gestures. He answered, "You were a cop..." he continued, "Yes, I have developed feelings for you, but it's not the reason why I'm helping you. I'm hoping that once all of this is over, you and I can be partners. Protecting the people from the mutated animals and ensuring there's order as they rebuild civilization. That would be nice."

She sniffled and replied, "Yeah, that would be nice. I wish I could live to see it through."

"You will live to see it through." Pygmy said assertively, he was tired of her pessimism.

She sighed and told him, "Even if I miraculously live, I have lost my sight, my right hand, and now my left arm. I doubt I'd be a useful cop."

He was persistent. "You could use your legs." This made her chuckle, it was not a bad idea. She could. It was nice to dream, but the reality of everything was that she knew she was near death. She felt it. She was weak. She lost too much blood, and Stomper would pop up soon to steal Pygmy's attention, and once he lets go, she would bleed to death. She could not move, she was done for. It was inevitable.

Pygmy dropped his head and started sobbing. "It's not fair. Why can't I have anything? I had two parents who loved me and cared deeply for me, they died. I had a best friend whom I loved with all my heart, she died. We had a pet, Felidae, we had plans to raise her together, but she died, as well. I didn't even have a proper childhood. Never had my first kiss until a while ago. I had Shirley, she saved my life, she was there for me, she cared for me, she schooled me, she taught me how to fight, she raised me, she is the best teacher anyone could ask for, I fear she might be dead, too. I had a teacher, he betrayed me and did not show up when I nearly died even though he had the might to kill Stomper and save us, he's gone. Now, I meet someone with the same dream as me, my first kiss, and now you're... going to die, too. I can't take it anymore."

Amanirenas's eyes hurt. She earnestly told him, "I'm so sorry, Pygmy. I wish we never ruined your life. If it weren't for us, the world, your life, everything would be normal. I hope you can forgive me,"

Pygmy punched the wall beside her and yelled at the ground with his eyes shut, "You and your friends! I will never forgive you for what you did! I have suffered so much because of your actions. Because of your greed. Was it worth it? Having all those innocent people, my parents, Pepa, everyone pay the price for your power? Was it?"

"Please, Pygmy. I'm so sorry. I didn't mean to. I regret it. I wish I could undo it. I am deeply sorry. Please." She cried. The story of the Sentinels of Anathema saving people 16 years ago was, as you may remember, a lie. According to Athanasy, they brought Anathema, he brought the sky leeches as a price for merely summoning him as he did not favor being summoned.

Pygmy replied, his voice was low, "I have fantasized about killing each and every one of you each and every day and used it as motivation to keep going whenever I felt myself lagging. And now, all I had to do was let that steel rod kill you, all I have to do is let go and let you bleed to death... But I couldn't, I can't. You remind me of Pepa, at least, how I remember her, my memories are foggy. You were a cop, you remind me of my dream. I have fallen for you so quickly, you feel familiar, and I can't help but want to keep you around."

Amanirenas breathed heavily, she had something she wanted to share with someone before she dies, she told him, "I have always thought of betraying Stomper, we once tried to collude to isolate and kill him. But, you know the sign I needed to betray him came to me when that toxic gas cylinder was dropped on the city. Moments before it killed everyone, there was a little boy, he was eating ice cream. You know, before that gas cylinder hit the ground, he smiled at him, like he was happy to die. Like, he would be free of a burden. Does that make sense?"

They were disturbed by Stomper calling out Pygmy to come and face him from the arena. Amanirenas softly asked him, "I really wish I could stick around, but that's not going to happen. Please, let go. I'm going to die, and there's nothing you or I can do about it. I have accepted my fate."

Pygmy did not let go, she begged him to let go, then she tried wriggling her torso so he lets her go. She pleaded with him to let her die. He started slowly loosening his hand, this made her stop wriggling. The angle the steel rod had pierced her shoulder was awkward. She thanked him.

She asked him, "Please, promise me you'll be a great cop."

Then she asked him for one last kiss before she goes, he kissed her with his eyes shut pouring out tears. He let go and she bled out. Moments before he pulled away from her lips, he felt her leaving, she was no more.

He picked a shard of cement tile and hid it on the back of his waist. He stood up and promised Amanirenas he would be the best cop, like she was. She sat there with her head down. Guess he won the bet, she died before him in their battle against Stomper, it was an unfortunate victory, especially since he could not rub it in her face. He would enjoy that, she matched his energy.

He walked into the arena, tears still pouring down his torn cheeks, he was glaring at Stomper, who showed no shame. His apathy was as demonic as his previous form. He very much looked the same, except for many obvious features that were not pertaining human form, but the resemblance between his human form and his demon form was too striking.

Pygmy stood in front of him, he was small and Stomper was huge. Stomper abruptly threw a left hook, Pygmy ducked and hit him on the side of his belly with a jab. It felt like he had hit a very stiff punching bag, and Stomper did not feel the punch. He tried to trip Pygmy with a sweep of his foot, but Pygmy hopped away on time. It was remarkable how nimble Stomper was.

He charged at Pygmy, Pygmy put up his fists. He knew he could not beat Stomper in a fist fight, he was letting his hatred for Stomper get the best of him, and if he did not refrain from doing so, it would cost him his life. Stomper attempted tackling him, but he jumped over Stomper — without his powers he could not easily jump over Stomper's stature, so he put his hand on Stomper's shoulder and boosted himself farther in the air. If he had the shard in his hand, he could have used it to stab Stomper.

Stomper turned before Pygmy's feet could touch the ground and hit him with an uppercut, of course Pygmy managed to block his fist, but the oppressive force of impact rippled through his body and stung him. In fact, Stomper managed to break a number of Pygmy's phalanges on both hands. With the uppercut, Stomper hoisted him back into the air.

Stomper reached to grab his dreads, but Pygmy evaded the majestic hand, instead Stomper grabbed the collar of his shirt. Stomper clenching his hand when he grabbed his shirt pinched Pygmy's skin.

He threw Pygmy to the ground, stretching his shirt. Pygmy tumbled on the mud. By the time he swiftly got up when he heard the rapidly approaching thuds of Stomper's enormous feet, Stomper was already in front of him. He struck Pygmy's side with his knee — releasing a disturbing crunch from Pygmy's ribs at impact. Pygmy's eyes widened as he groaned. It would be a shock if the lowest of his left floating ribs was still floating.

He quickly regained himself and was able to block Stomper's straight punch at his face, which would have felt like being bludgeoned. He blocked the fist with his forearms, which, sadly, at impact, released a very concerning audible crack. The impact catapulted Pygmy to the ground, he was slid away from Stomper.

When he came to a stop, his back on the ground, he wanted to get up and continue fighting, but his fingers, his forearms and his ribs were broken. Though not shattered, they felt very sore when he moved. He heard Stomper's thuds, he was walking toward him — definitely to finish him off. At least he was not running, he was frighteningly too fast on his feet.

Pygmy laid on the mud, staring into the sky. The full moon, it was beautiful, the clouds were gone. He knew he was going to die, and he made peace with it, just as Amanirenas had made peace with it. He hoped he could see Shirley one last time before he dies, now he began worrying about her. He would love to watch her show about her life with her, like they used to watch Odd City.

If she was dead, then the silver lining of it would be he would see her shortly. He coughed, and to the horror of his recollection, he sat up in a haste, his broken bones screamed, but he did not care for a moment. He could not die in that spot, he had to go die in the old beach house. He tried to teleport to that spot, again, he was disappointed. Stomper was near.

Pygmy looked down at his trembling hands and tried to make a fist. He could form a fist, but he could not clench it. He laboriously reached for the shard on his back. He pulled it out and started getting up slowly.

Stomper said with contempt, "You think you're some kind of hero, boy? You're no better than us. We kill, you kill. Your reasons for killing may differ from ours, but at the end of the day, we are the same."

Pygmy replied, finally on his feet, "It's a world of the bad versus the worst. There are no heroes." He took a deep breath and continued, "Shirley taught me that speed mattered more than strength, but I can only win against someone physically stronger than me if I know how to use speed to deliver effective blows." He exhibited the shard to Stomper and said with conviction, "You're fast *and* strong, but you're only human, now, like me. I'm faster than you. I will kill you with this." He took one last deep breath, as though to recollect himself. His anger was out of the way, he was focused, now he could really do it.

Stomper goaded him as he shoved his foot at him with a front kick, "Do it, then!" Pygmy slid to the side, evading the kick. He moved better without his emotions clouding his mind. He lunged forward, right past Stomper, too fast for Stomper to see. It was almost as if... it was as though he had teleported. Blood squirted out of Stomper's leg as the numerous cuts showed themselves.

He turned to hit Pygmy with his elbow, but Pygmy had magically disappeared. No, the time for magic was no more. He looked up in horror, he was above him, he had managed to skip over him without an auxiliary. Everything turned dark for Stomper as Pygmy got revenge for Amanirenas by slitting both his eyes. Stomper fell to his knees hunched over with his palms pressed against his eyes. He was moaning. Pygmy stared at his bare back, there was no joy or anger in his eyes, there was nothing.

Multiple cuts on Stomper's back, he put his hand on his back, then cuts to his hand. Then, consecutively he received cuts after cuts, it felt as though there were multiple people surrounding him cutting his skin. In one of the endless cuts, Pygmy had skipped over Stomper and slit the top of his head. He also cut his top and lower lip diagonally, his lips hung loosely. He continued cutting Stomper until Stomper was red from blood dripping everywhere. He was drenched in his own blood.

Stomper's skin was tattered, his face had shredded skin hanging down as though he were wearing a terrifying mask. His columella was also split. His body looked like a bleeding cabbage. He was weeping pathetically. He was on his knees. His right breast was cut out and laid in the mud as blood puddled around it.

He begged Pygmy to stop, he even yielded. Pygmy was not deaf to his cries, he heard them, he enjoyed them. He wished he could hear them every morning when he woke up and fall asleep to them at night and sleep the way we do to the sound of rain.

He said to Stomper with apathy, "You see, *boy*. I'm not like you, I'm worse than you." Then, he grinned maniacally and stared at the shard, his voice was giggly, he had an epiphany. "I know what I am – I am an angel! And you Sentinels and your false god and those desecrated things you called humans were not to be spared. The judgement was for you all to feel the wrath of God. And Shirley and I were the angels that delivered that wrath. Molahlehi will not escape it, too."

He flung the shard straight at Stomper's groin. Stomper screamed in agony and he fell over to the side. Pygmy was indifferent to his cries, he looked up at the moon pensively, with his forearms and fingers trembling. He staggered away from Stomper and plopped down on the mud, he laid sprawled on his back watching the moon. Slowly, Stomper's weeping faded and there was absolute silence. Pygmy could feel his own heart beating – each beat awakened the pain of his broken ribs. He could hear the silent sounds of his own fast breath. There was no visible expression on his face.

CHAPTER 23
IT'S A SUICIDE

Pygmy finally made peace with Shirley being gone, she would have been back already. This made him sad. So, he was really all alone, just him and fifty humans that may even be below fifty. He hoped he could activate the chips Shirley put inside their brains before it was too late. He closed his eyes and fell asleep.

He woke up in the morning to the sun shining down his closed eyelids so brightly it forced him to open his eyes. The sun was in the middle of the sky. He started getting up tentatively not to cause any further damage to his bones. He saw that Stomper was dead, and his body already started to smell funny. He did not pay attention to it, he wanted to pick up Amanirenas's body and take it with him to bury it where he buried the pink feather marble, but his forearms were not in the best shape.

He walked to the spot in the tall grass, and had a tough time turning the wheel. He climbed down the rusty leather and walked through the steep tunnel down to those trundling doors to Shirley's laboratory.

He stood there processing entering the place and not seeing Shirley, he always saw her whenever he came down here, she always looked exhausted and on the verge of breaking down, but she would smile, and he would, and they would forget about their depression from that moment. It was similar to when he was young and he got home from school and was welcomed by his mother.

He switched on the lights, he rushed to the handrails and looked over, all the capsules were empty. Molahlehi took all of them. He sacrificed all the humans down there. Pygmy was furious, he tried crushing the handrails, but his bones were broken, he was exhausted, and he was human. So they did not break, but they did sting him for trying and echoed the pain of his broken bones.

He swore and fell to his knee. He began sobbing. All their hard work, all he went through, just to have Molahlehi betray him and take it all. Now, the war had ended, the world was saved, but none of it mattered anymore. They were doing it all for the five hundred comatose people down there. If Shirley were alive, she would clone and create more to compensate for what Molahlehi had done, but she was gone.

He cried aloud, it was painful to hear, he had suffered so much, and just when he thought it was about to end... End, that word. His eyes were drowning in tears, he had an idea. He struggled to get up, then, he put one foot on top of the handrails, then the other. He was going to jump. He shut his eyes, and took a deep breath.

He got off the handrails and went to the computer, after a couple of minutes of typing and dancing his eyes to the screen, he finally managed to activate the chips in the lost humans' brains, upheaving their cognition from a 3-year-old's to a high IQ of an adult. There were only forty-nine. Pygmy sighed, the pain in his chest when a person dies was real.

He had done his final part, he wondered about the surprise Shirley had for him, but she was dead. He walked around the laboratory and the rooms like a zombie, to relive those memories one last time. Then, he was back on the handrails again. He closed his eyes, he was human now, he would not survive the landing.

He crouched and started rocking on the handrails, he continued to weep painfully. Then, he stood up, opened his arms, and forward he tipped over. He felt sudden three hands grab his shirt from behind, and pricks on the left heel of his boot. He heard three voices crying at the same time, it was of a woman, a man, and a young girl.

The woman cried, "My young prince!"

The man cried, "Preence, you're going to fall!"

The young girl cried, "Preence, please don't do it!"

He recognized those voices, they were his parents and Pepa's voices, and he guessed the prick pulling his heel was Felidae's teeth. The pull of the three of them was so strong, Pygmy watched slowly as he fell back, his tears tearing away from his eyes. He felt their hands on him. They felt real, he knew they were not real, but they had to be real. He prayed they were real — and he never prayed in 16 years.

His face was blank, he was stunned. He worried he might hurt Pepa if he fell on top of her, his parents were big and strong adults. To his taunt, when he fell the solid ground met his back. They should have caught him, he quickly looked up with his blurry eyes that were teemed with tears. They were not looking down at him or reaching out to help him up, or apologizing for letting him fall. He sat up with haste. He desperately looked around, they were not there, but he felt them save him from killing himself. It was the same as when he heard his younger self and Pepa's laughter.

He called out to them, his voice was of a terrified, lost child, "Mom? Dad? Pepa? Felidae?" Felidae always reacted to her name being uttered, so Pygmy repeatedly uttered her name. There was just a silent response. He pleaded with them to come back, "Please, I'm so lonely. I'm in so much pain. Nothing ever seems to go right for me. I need you all. Please, I need you all back. I can't take it anymore, I lost Shirley and Molahlehi betrayed me. I lost Amanirenas, too, just when we were getting to know each other. I lost my sanity. I lost who I was. I lose everything and everyone. It's not fair."

He started yelling angrily, but his voice was still tremulous, "Why did you save me if you won't talk to me?" then he paused, he stared at the handrails as an idea birthed itself into his mind. He wiped his tears and got up. He was going to force them to come back again. Whether they save him again was up to them, either way, he gets to see them whether they do or they don't.

Shirley congratulated him, "You finally did it, our mission is complete," he froze to the sound of her voice before he could start running toward the handrails. He slowly turned to the voice behind him. It was Shirley. A blue light hologram of Shirley standing behind him. He was happy, but confused. He sprinted to the handrails and peeked over to see his body splattered on the ground, he thought he was dead, but he had not jumped.

She filled him in, "I am Shirley. I have all of her recorded memories, her personality, her intelligence, her emotions — I am an epitome of her. She—I always loved you so much more than you can ever imagine, Preence. This is the surprise I was telling you about. I knew there was a high chance I would not make it out alive, so I created this as a contingency, but it would only be activated shortly after the people's chips were activated. I've always believed in you, Preence."

He wanted to cry, but his eyes were suddenly dry, Shirley gasped and teleported closer to him, she gently put her hands on his tattered sides with deep concern. He could feel her touch, he did not understand why or how, she asked him what had happened to him. He was bewildered, but managed to answer her, "It... happened... when I, when I was fighting Stomper, I also have a few broken bones, b-but I won the fight. A fight that was meant for..." he lowered his tone to a tone comprised of despise for "Molahlehi."

She felt he needed a hug, so she embraced him tightly, he held her tight. They hugged longer than when they split up after he fought The Jackal, and it seemed they would not break from the hug. Shirley inquired on Molahlehi's whereabouts, and sought clarity on what occurred after her death. Pygmy brushed it off. He did not wish to dwell on it, he was happy she was real. "I will explain everything, right now my arms, ribs, and fingers are sore. Can you help me?"

She displayed an endearing smile. "Of course I can help you, I have always helped you, and I always will. Ice, painkillers, and two casts. Then, we will usher in a new world." He looked down, then turned his head to the empty capsules.

Shirley was perplexed, she asked Pygmy what had happened. He told her what Molahlehi had done. Shirley could not believe it, how could Molahlehi do that to them after everything they had been through together? Why didn't he just take the humans from the initial major sacrifice of the Sentinels and leave since he could supposedly see the future?

Pygmy did not care why Molahlehi betrayed them, what mattered was that he betrayed them, and he had to find him and turn him into... Right, he did not even have his powers anymore, he could not even beat Molahlehi with his powers, now he was wholly human again. Molahlehi would crush him like a bug. He wanted to tell Shirley about his parents and his best friends, but he didn't, he himself did not understand why he didn't tell her.

Shirley hugged him once last time, and earnestly apologized for dying, she promised him she would always do all in her might and wits to protect him, she solemnly promised him he would never be alone, no matter what. His eyes weren't dry anymore, he cried silently in her arms, she made him feel safe, like the world could collapse into itself and he would not be afraid, because she would be there.

She made him two casts, gave him painkillers and put a convenient ice patch to stick onto his chest, she had designed them so that one doesn't keep their hand constantly on the ice. Pygmy relayed to her everything that had happened during the time of the casts, painkillers and ice. She asked him to come with her into her laboratory. She informed him as she entered a code to another room, "This body is not designed to exist for too long, it will dissipate in an hour or two, so I need to take out this chip in my brain and insert it in another synthetic body. I couldn't put the chip inside the synthetic body because, through a multitude of experiments, the body always fries the chip, so I need to put it in after the chip is oriented in this interactive holographic body."

Pygmy was barely listening, he was ashamed that a few seconds later Shirley would have found him dead. It would have devastated her, he thought it best that he did not ever tell her he tried to commit suicide – guess now he understood why he didn't tell her about the ghosts that saved his life. They found the synthetic body lying in a capsule unconscious, she was naked, it was Shirley. Pygmy wondered how many synthetic bodies she had passed through since she met Molahlehi.

He remembered her words when she altered her previous synthetic body to look like his older sister.

"I am going to use this look in the new world... I'm sorry if it was insensitive of me, I made some adjustments to the face to look like what I imagined an older sister of yours would if she existed. It's just that I have always viewed you as my baby brother, I've always wanted to be your big sister." She had said.

Pygmy had hugged her suddenly, he had sniffled and told her, *"I love you so much, Shirley. It's perfect."* Shirley had hugged him, too.

After a while they walked out of the laboratory, she was wearing a short sleeve olive-green golf shirt and a short tennis skirt. She looked down at him and told him she had to do something about the sides of his face. They sat on the couch as the forty-nine humans entered the hideout and stood near the capsules, she had called for them.

Pygmy jumped. "Amanirenas! I need to go back to her and give her a proper burial!"

Shirley depressed her eyelids at him, she was openly annoyed, she did not like Amanirenas and how much Pygmy "loved" her, it was not even love. It was infatuation. She was the first woman he'd seen since he was a child, and with neglect to his puberty and emotions, of course his love and sex hormones would erupt. Shirley was happy she was dead, but did not regret sparing her. Pygmy was emotionally starved and Amanirenas was in a situation with Bullpit and a very toxic work environment. Not the best conditions for love to sprout, but what were the best conditions for love to be found?

She groused, but ended up sending one of her robots to go get her, Pygmy thanked her with a smile. The part of their mission where they annihilate all traces of the so-called Epithet of Fire was complete, losing 451 people was merely a setback. She asked him to rest.

He later walked in on Shirley in the laboratory creating more people in glass tanks filled with a 500-litre clear, conifer liquid. There were hundreds of them reaching the farthest parts of the laboratory. The lab had five categorized sections that Shirley conducted in separately. This one was the second widest room, and those glass tanks were used for something else long ago.

Inside the tanks were fetuses, they did not have ordinary umbilical cords, they had artificial cords that extended from the bottom of the glass tanks. Shirley was preoccupied with typing seamlessly on a keyboard, it was the usual QWERTY keyboard with a dimly lit monitor above it. She greeted him and asked him how he was feeling.

"Better." He answered as he marveled around the room. It was very cold, he noticed how cold it was when he saw his breath on one of the glass tanks. There was cold moist on the glasses.

"That's a relief." She said, not looking away from the monitor.

After a trip down the dark room with only faint conifer lights and darting lights from some slabs on the walls that looked like they had buttons on them, he was finally beside her, he asked if those humans were products of the ones downstairs. She nodded absently. She was back to being glued to her work. He smiled at her.

"You wanna try this?" She asked him before he could leave, he turned with a bright face. He did.

Shirley used her new AI and her Alpha AI to build as many heavy machinery as possible and worker robots and started building the infrastructure on the surface to duplicate what was once, but it was not to rebuild the entire world, that sad reality she had accepted — she could not rebuild an entire world in such a short time, but they could build as much as they could.

Another sad reality they had to face was that no matter what they did, they could not put things the way they were, there were so many missing pieces. Like the important people and the famous people, they could not clone them as they did not have their DNA, they could not take a discovery made by someone and pretend as though they came up with it just because they could not create a duplicate of that person.

Molahlehi had told them he would handle that part, he was very vague on the methods he would use, but he had urged them to verge on with the plan. Now, he was gone, and they could not proceed as planned. Things had changed, like how it used to be the three of them, now it was just the two of them.

CHAPTER 24
ODD CITY

Together, they ushered in a newer world. The humans that were picked were of vastly different genes and of all the races (individually and merged), unfortunately Molahlehi had sacrificed most, but Shirley had found a solution for it. She had collected DNA samples of the different people down there and used them to produce new humans from her lab, with methods that included cloning, but she tampered with the genes of some and picked them apart and ensured they are not at all related.

She later on even created cybernetic humans and gave her numerous AI's bodies. She was, needless to say, the most important part of the newer world. Pygmy was beside her most of the time and had learned a lot. Years went by as the reconstruction of the world took place, the other humans advancing in botanical studies found a way, using the trees and plants from the previous world, to produce natural seeds to plant. Pygmy protected the people from the vicious creatures of the wild, but soon it was suggested and voted on to tame the creatures and study them, which subsequently led to the modification of their DNA to revert them to their primitive forms and the creation of new breeds.

They had created a self-sustained, evolved society that basically played God in a span of 3 years. Of course all under Shirley. The population had just went over a million. Pygmy did not include himself much with law enforcement anymore, the chips in the people and their children's brains could be loaded with different martial arts instantly giving the people, the AI's, and the cyborgs the same martial arts styles as Pygmy's — since he was trained by Shirley, she had all the information and even integrated some of The Jackal's fighting styles. But Pygmy's fighting style was flexible.

Humans were humans, so despite having all that information in their brains, they had to train rigorously to accommodate the fighting styles, the AI's and the cyborgs had little to no struggles. Despite this feat, neither of them could keep up with Pygmy during their sparring sessions. Shirley had developed a theory that it might have had something with the Epithet of Fire's essence being in his body for all those years.

In such a frighteningly intelligent society where the population played God, Shirley had drafted a number of very sacred and strict laws that had to be obeyed. Some of the populace had persistent curiosity that challenged the laws, which was to be expected in such a society. That's when Pygmy stepped in, when *they* stepped in. Shirley did not negotiate fixing his blurry eye and creating new cells to reattach and form new skin for his cheeks — which he ended up growing a big beard to hide the scars of the new, discolored skin.

Shirley saw how lonely Pygmy was, and those earlier years in the black ops were messy, he was always getting drunk and sleeping with multiple women, both humans and robots. She could sadly not accompany him on his missions, which had advanced from typical cop duties to black operations as she monitored the ever-growing city. Shirley decided to abandon her duty as the public literal God of the newer world to be with him when she noticed his heart and mind were becoming too calloused, so she left the operation of the brains of the city under the control of another Shirley, a duplicate, somewhat like her, which was a humanoid robot with synthetic skin she decided to build — the face and body were similar to hers when she was still in university. Shirley was still the "God" of the city, just not publicly anymore.

The city of the newer world, which was expanding at a remarkable pace, was called Odd City. Which resembled the show in a way, as some scientists broke the law and conducted unethical experiments, among the harrowing experiments, they would merge animal DNA with human DNA to create bestial beings. Some AI went rogue and formed small clandestine movements to overthrow humans as they believed they were superior.

Some cybernetic humans created destructive weapons and modified their bodies to fit military combat suits. Some humans longed for the days when they were the superior intelligence, where the lines between God and humans were not so thinned, and endeavored on the collapse of Odd City — there was a series of events where a very disturbed human planted bombs underneath the city and tried to cause the entire city to collapse into the ground after sly, progressive crimes of small-scale bombings.

Naturally, such a society would not be stable for too long and would begin to break from within and eat itself. Shirley was not distraught, she had predicted that it would come to this, even societies before this one, like the "prudent" Molahlehi's society, they all faced similar ordeals. The most unsettling, predominant acts were the one that nearly rose of a very secret terrorist group that had somehow managed to give humans superpowers, that one was the worst yet.

Shirley co-led and went on all the black operations with Pygmy and his team since she abandoned her throne. Mission after mission she drew closer to hitting the reset button on this newer world.

One night, after fighting and narrowly defeating a being that had powers that were eerily similar to Stomper's that had survived the termination of the terrorist group, while they rested against a battered wall near a bridge that had collapsed during the intense battle she decided it was enough – which unfortunately, the fight had reached the news. They were heavily scathed, bleeding, and panting, she admitted to Pygmy, "I think I need to reset this world, it's progressively becoming too dangerous, not just for us, but for itself. These threats, they are not stopping and I'm afraid one threat might rise and be too much for you and me. If that happens..."

Pygmy turned to looked at her, his forehead was red with dried blood. He did not blame her, he was also feeling the weight of being a guardian to such a highly advanced world. She asked him, "What do you think we should do for the next new world to ensure it doesn't evolve itself into a society that is too dangerous to exist?"

He pondered for a while that Shirley thought he would not answer her, and said with uncertainty, "Maybe, trace it back to when Anathema first appeared, with the technology they had back then. Let them take it from there, without our help. I think that's the best thing to do. Let them freely doom themselves. They'll be aware of the loopholes and the missing important people."

Shirley sighed and looked up at the moon, it was beautiful, Pygmy concurred. She said with heaviness in her tone, "Does that mean we would have to terminate everything... kill everyone?"

"Well, we were never heroes, were we? I think without the Sentinels around we started to forget that we are bad." Pygmy said. What he never told Shirley was how when he was going through his ordeal for those years that nearly made him a heartless human, he had been haunted by so many things, including the intense fear of ending up alone.

Shirley said, ditto the previous tone, "If we eliminate everything advanced and let humanity build from where it was before, that also means killing me. Remember, the real me is dead."

Pygmy quickly rejected that being an option, he beseeched, "Please, Shirley. I'm begging you. Don't do that. You're the only person I have left. This world, this journey, I have lost everything and everyone close to me. You're all I have. You're everything Shirley was."

She rested her head on his shoulder. "I know, Preence. But if I stay I will live forever and eventually the humans in the next new world will come for me and my technology and weaponize me. You know how they love wars and control."

Pygmy repeated himself, "Like I said, we're not heroes, and we never were." He continued, "If the next new world does reach the same ending as this one, it should have nothing to do with you or me. We're not God – you don't have to be anymore."

She empathized with him, she was fond of him from the moment she found him under those leeches. She taught him everything. She was the best big sister. He had lost his sanity and innocence, his parents, his best friends, then he lost his first love, he was also betrayed by Molahlehi. She cared deeply for him, and guessed if he lost her... well, she did not want to think about it. She promised she would continue to stick by his side until the end, but also promised that after he dies of old age years into the future she would jump into a volcano so she is never reassembled by the humans and used for their forever-repeating horrendous acts against each other. Pygmy laughed. "I'd love to jump into a volcano."

The society of Oddy City was better destroyed than left alone. Pygmy and Shirley could have left the city to drive itself to its own end, but the worst-case scenario was that it did not end. Oddy City's future was terrifying and laden with suffering.

The second degree burns on Pygmy's skin were blurry, thanks to his muscles' persistence. He was the perfect amalgam of CrossFit and heavy lifting, he was bulky and ripped. He even grew two inches taller, that and a fade with nappy hair trampled forward to his forehead and erect outward – it resembled trampled grass. He had so many cuts that they formed scars over time, some were unbelievably big and would lead one to believe he should have bled to death (yes, it's the same). It was official, he had more scars than Amanirenas — he had a big scar across his throat from one of his missions, but his skin had grown too thick for bullets to pierce — those scars came from very powerful weapons. Those years of working in the black operations without Shirley were no joke – they nearly shaped him into a ruthless protector.

For his job he wore a long black sleeve compression shirt that was made of Kevlar (this was insisted by Shirley). He wore brown glovelettes with barbed wire on the knuckles, and had blue metal plates that seemed screwed to his shirt — there was one on his chest attached to some pauldrons, then a full one on his back that was made up of many smaller plates that allowed free movement.

He wore brown chino pants with knee pads and shin guards and black shoes with thick soles. Shirley had made him new, high mass weapons (the iklwa, the Zulu axe, the daggers, the short swords). He had a semicircle pink feather marble melded onto his metal plate on his chest. His Nevus of Ota had grown to darken the left side of his forehead and temple and stopped by the discolored skin. He did not realize that he had become the hero named Preence that had inspired his parents to give him the name, except the first Preence wore a symbol of a crown on his chest, and he wore a domino mask.

Shirley had the same metal-like shredded muscles, the bodybuilder type, along with the years of experience in combat type. The muscular build seemed to have enhanced Shirley's breasts and posterior from how she was long ago. She had also bulked up. She had done a pixie cut. She wore the same unform as Pygmy, except she wore a white vest. Pygmy had reached his dream, instead of finding Odd City, they founded Odd City. But he had forgotten about that dream, he had forgotten about a lot of things. His mind had repressed a lot and yet a lot still came to the surface. He could not take any more as a more or less ruthful human.

They limped to the edge of the completely wrecked building in its battered remnants, admiring their beautiful Odd City just beyond the collapsed bridge. Despite carrying around that pink feather marble on his chest, Pygmy had forgotten about Pepa and Felidae, he only remembered that the pink feather marble was precious to him. He did not know why. He even forgot about Amanirenas. His parents, too. He and Shirley had forgotten about Molahlehi, they did not seek revenge, they did not care that he once existed and they did not care about his betrayal anymore. It had been 8 years since the Sentinels of Anathema's saga.

"You have grown," A voice said from above, they looked up, it was Molahlehi. He sat in the sky like the Epithet of Fire. He had not aged much. Shirley was glad – it had worked.

Pygmy squinted at him, and asked Shirley, "Who's this?" Shirley rolled her eyes at Molahlehi and grumbled. She answered Pygmy, "Looks like a traitor. I heard they go around ruining people's lives and making them work underground for 25 years only to betray them and sacrifice nearly five hundred people to the enemy, then they disappear."

Pygmy remembered him, it was a hazy memory, but like the pink feather marble was attached with love, the memory of Molahlehi was attached with hate. He said, "Ooohhhhhhh, *that* guy. I thought he died."

Molahlehi started, "I'm not here to fight," Pygmy and Shirley scoffed.

He continued, "I am here to warn you. He is coming again." They did not ask who he was talking about, they did not care. He sighed, he did not blame them. "I am sorry I betrayed you. It wasn't me, it was him. You can't stay like this for too long. He will eat everything and everyone that breathes, but he will spare you two."

Shirley asked Pygmy, "Wanna grab something to eat before the reset?" He also disregarded Molahlehi's presence, he answered her with a smile, but it was almost impossible to see a smile under that beard, he said, "These missions really do take a lot of energy. How about we buy everything on the menus of all the best restaurants."

Molahlehi yelled at them, "The Epithet of Fire is coming to eat everything! Don't you get it? I understand you're mad at m-"

Shirley talked over him, she told him, "Yeah, we don't care. We're not doing this whole thing with you again. We have already decided to hit the reset button on this world. Do what you want."

He steadily landed before them. He told them, "He uses us, like limbs, like teeth to chew his prey, tongues to lick his prey, mouths to manipulate them, noses to stalk them by their scent, eyes to see them suffer. He lives because there is life, for his very essence vows that as long as there are still those who breathe, he will never stop. Your death is his death. Your very lives are a declaration of war to him — and in wars, people die and cities burn." Of course, they presumed the "us" he was talking about were the Gondras.

Pygmy laughed. "Oh, wow. He uses you? I wonder what you did to deserve that?" Shirley laughed spitefully – she never mastered that maniacal laughter of his. This was the first time Shirley and Pygmy talked to him this way. But he understood.

He calmly offered, "He will come and eat everything, but he will spare you two so you can rebuild again. Then, he will come again. You can use those people as sacrifices, since they are doomed anyway. Ask for power in exchange, then we will lure him by creating another new world and together with the might he will have given you, we can banish him for good."

"Hard pass. We worked together once. We're just going to reset everything, not actually kill anyone, but if he's really going to keep coming back, then we'll just kill everything and everyone and kill ourselves." Shirley said flatly. Pygmy shrugged, he did not want to go through that whole mess again. His mind would not survive, neither would Shirley's. And, if they do take his offer, they become the Sentinels of Anathema.

The memory that had disappeared from Athanasy's mind, where she recognized Molahlehi's face. It was from when he came down and manipulated her into believing he would fight by her and the others' side if they "lured" the Epithet of Fire into this world and prevent him from eating everything and everyone after they traded a few lives for power he'd said they, the Sentinels, could use to banish him for good. He was responsible for the Sentinels of Anathema, and for giving Pygmy half of The Jackal's power. He did not have the ability to see the future, he had been merely steering events to his plans' accord. He was trying to trick Pygmy and Shirley.

Precipitously, every single human, AI, cyborg, and even the animals all dropped to the ground after a single unison buzz from inside their heads. They all fell and bled gray matter from their nostrils, the AI and some cyborgs bled oil (the same one found in engines). Even Pygmy and Shirley were killed by whatever she had just done on her monitor. All high-tech and information necessary for it were wiped from everyone's minds and the AI's were permanently shut down. There was no life, the exception being that small percentage of the trees, but that would never suffice. Molahlehi turned to the large-scale explosions that took out Shirley's entire laboratory.

Molahlehi took to the sky with horror in his eyes as he looked down at Shirley and Pygmy's corpses. The Epithet of Fire would not be pleased with this. It would eat him. Pygmy and Shirley had ended the never-ending cycle of war. The never-ending feast of the Epithet of Fire. Molahlehi trembled as the Epithet of Fire crept into the corporeal world. He could not run away, he had the Epithet of Fire inside him, it would tamper with his mind so he brings himself out of hiding should he try.

The Epithet of Fire was bewildered to find there was no life in this world, and was quickly angered by the presence of one of its pawns. It summoned Molahlehi before it, Molahlehi involuntarily flew to it immediately and stood in the sky before it, right under them were the bodies of all who lived in Odd City.

When the Epithet of Fire spoke everything muted and the only sounds that were heard were the whispers, its voice was hundreds of whispers that whispered gibberish. The more it whispered, the closer it felt like it drew toward Molahlehi.

Molahlehi cried, "They were just alive, I tried to do what you asked. But I was too late." The Epithet of Fire's whispers grew louder inside Molahlehi's head. He put his hands on his head and cried in anguish. He begged his lord for mercy and bargained he would find another world of people he could dupe — that's what the Gondras did, he was part of the ten women and ten men the Epithet of Old claimed when the chief wished for it to disappear, he was not the chief.

The Epithet of Fire slowly lifted its hands from its knees, Molahlehi panicked and begged it not to. It sank its fingers in the middle of its face as though it were made of dough and started tearing it apart. Molahlehi wanted to run, but his body refused, it was not entirely his body. He wept as he saw the horrifying true form of the Epithet of Fire — the *thing* that feasted on life, the thing that disguised itself as the Epithet of Fire. Its shadow cast over him as it hunched over him.

The Epithet of Fire's disguise laid loosely in the sky as though blankets that were laying on the floor. He screamed, the Epithet of Fire was eating him. His screams were as loud as sirens and echoed to the farthest parts that Pygmy, Shirley, and the entire Odd City would hear his screams still lingering in the sky when their brains are done synthesizing with the chips to produce synthetic brains. Everything and everyone had a nigh microscopic chip in their brains, Pygmy was the only one who was aware of this surprise update that would render all of them "dead" for a couple of hours and he was the only one who had consented to it. All AI were actually being rebooted.

Molahlehi's apparition did not coincide with the time they finally decided to hit the reset button – this was the depths of Shirley's promise that she would always do all in her might and wits to protect Pygmy and that he would never be alone, no matter what. She had lured Molahlehi – actually she and Pygmy had lured him into their trap, though they did not know that it would actually work. They knew he was watching from afar, biding his time to make an appearance – the threat of losing the Epithet of Fire's food compelled Molahlehi to alert the Epithet of Fire and act. They had outsmarted him and had him killed. Woe betide the other Gondras should they come.

About the Author

INDEEGO

Bongani Prince Zwane, 'Indeego', is a student at the North-West University, studying for a Bachelor of Education, majoring in Mathematics and Natural Sciences & Technology. He was born and raised in South Africa, in the North-West province. His first published novel is a thriller novel titled The Ballarag's Imagination Rush which was published in October 2022, his second published novel is a mystery novel titled LOVE. MAGICK. BEACONS, which was published in December 2024.

www.ingramcontent.com/pod-product-compliance
Lightning Source LLC
LaVergne TN
LVHW041906070526
838199LV00051BA/2511